Other books by the author:

Calamity (poetry) chapbook
living must bury (poetry)

The Galaxie
and Other Rides

Josie Sigler

Livingston Press
The University of West Alabama

isbn 13: 978-1-60489-097-6 library binding
isbn 13: 978-1-60489-098-3 trade paper
Library of Congress Control Number 2012930429
Printed on acid-free paper.
Printed in the United States of America by
United Graphics

Hardcover binding by: Heckman Bindery
Typesetting and page layout: Joe Taylor
Cover design: Jana Vukovic
Author photo: Jennifer Sibara

Grateful thanks to the editors of the publications listed below for first
publishing the following stories:

"Deep, Michigan" appeared in *Water-Stone Review*, 2008.

"The Black Box" appeared in *Copper Nickel Review*, 2008.

"My Last Horse" appeared in *Silk Road*, 2009.

"Breakneck Road" appeared in *Silk Road*, 2010.

"El Camino" appeared in *Roanoke Review*, 2010.

"A Man Is Not a Star" appeared in *Hunger Mountain*, 2011.

"Even the Crocuses" appeared in *The Ledge Poetry and Fiction Magazine*, 2012.

**This collection won the Tartt First Fiction Award,
which is sponsored by the President's Office at UWA.**

first edition

6 5 4 3 3 2 1

for my dad, George John Sigler, who taught me about cars

and for Sheila O'Connor, who taught me about stories

CONTENTS

I don't even like old cars. I mean they don't even interest me. I'd rather have a goddam horse. A horse is at least human, for God's sake.

—J.D. Salinger, *The Catcher in the Rye*

Pull the curtains back and look outside,
somebody somewhere don't know.
Come on now child, we're gonna go for a ride,
car wheels on a gravel road.

—Lucinda Williams, "Car Wheels on a Gravel Road"

The Galaxie and Other Rides

DEEP, MICHIGAN
[*Caprice*]

Richie was the only one who had enough credits to graduate because he took all the retard classes. The rest of us failed English again. So the day of the ceremony, everybody else in their caps and gowns, Little Ho boosts Mrs. Hendrick's piece-of-shit '77 Caprice out of the school parking lot and drives us all up to Caseville Beach.

Actually it's my idea, me who says, Let's steal her goddamned car.

We're sitting on Rochelle's front porch loading up for the day. The beer nestled in my nuts is already warm though it's only ten in the morning.

Yeah, you guys need another car for sure, Rochelle says, rolling her eyes at her mother's driveway, where our rustbuckets are lined up like it's a fricking parade. Rochelle's the only girl we hang with, and she tries to keep us in line, too.

But Little Ho gets what I mean right away. He sees it's the principle of the thing.

Rochelle says, Don't be stupid, Ho, though she knows it's a lost cause. She started sitting against the fence on the playground with The Ho right around the time his mom died. That was sixth grade. Not a one of us can see how a faggot like The Ho landed a girl like her, but this is the shit that happens. And of course she won't come with us up to Caseville.

So I'm really the one who calls the Caprice, and Richie's the one who goes over to the parking lot and hot-wires it, which he can do because he has the cap and gown. And Ball's the one who wants to drive so far up into the freaking Thumb. But The Ho does the driving because he's the only one sober.

All the way the radio is stuck on the oldies station but we don't even care. We sing along to Creedence Clearwater Revival and we're feeling pretty good.

The beach is almost empty because everyone in goddamned Michigan is graduating from somewhere except us, and I know my grandma's at home cussing my name. But the sky there in Caseville is blue and the sun feels so good that even Ball takes off his shirt. We rest on our backs in the sand until we feel ourselves sinking into it, forgetting who we are, a bunch of losers from Deep, Michigan, who can't pass English.

And of course the cops show up. No reason except bad luck. As soon as Richie sees them, he books it all the way down to the breakwater. Richie would get killed in jail, either that or he'd kill someone like that retarded guy Lenny in the book Mrs. Hendrick gave us to read last year. I stole that book, though I don't usually steal. I took it after she looked up at me from behind her big metal desk and said, You know you could go to college if you applied yourself. I used to get straight A's, it's true, but that was way back in freshman year.

Anyway, the cops sniff around the car the way they do while we decide whether to run like retards, too. Like goddamned cowards. Though now I wish we had.

The cops come all the way down to the water in their stiff grey pants. They start asking us whether we're from Deep and whether we know a certain Ms. Hendrick. The tall, skinny one is obviously a faggot. He lisps Msssss and stares at The Ho's muscles that twitch and shine all sweaty when he steps forward.

The Ho takes the rap for me and Ball because we're already eighteen and he's still got six months. He says we don't know the car is stolen. He stole it by himself. And we know right then he's going to juvey one more time. Maybe for a month or two.

But when the cops search the car, they find the .357 Magnum

buried in The Ho's duffel bag.

What the fuck? I say.

The cops scowl at my *fuck* like somebody's mother's standing there with us.

Chuchie. Jesus. It's my *dad's*.

As if that explains it all.

They take Little Ho to the car in his soggy Bermuda shorts, sand still clinging in the low divots of his sun-brown back as they cuff him.

They make us ride home with them, too, because we can't ride back in Mrs. Hendrick's car. Ball is freaking out the whole time, crying in the backseat, curled as much as he can curl so that The Ho and I have somewhere to put our asses. And of course, the cops, brilliant like they are, never even notice Richie, even though he's waving from the breakwater as the car pulls away, his green gown billowing around him. We can see his big rectangle mouth is open and we know he's scared.

The Ho and I are silent. I put my hand behind him and feel past the cuffs, and he grips my fingers all the way to Deep.

My grandma almost shits herself seeing me get out of that cop car. And I know she'll shit twice if she catches me going out again as soon as she's asleep, but someone has to get Richie. I push my bike a goddamned mile before I start it so she won't hear. And then I drive two hours north to snag Richie's retarded ass and drop him home with Ball. Just before dawn I head to Rochelle's to tell her what happened.

I climb in her window, which we've been doing for years. Whenever my grandma kicks me out or The Ho's dad goes on a rampage, we hide out at Rochelle's. Her mom'll feed you burritos and put you on the couch and she'll wake you up on time for work or she'll even bring you a blanket if you want to sleep on Rochelle's floor.

Rochelle starts to stir and I sit on the edge of her bed and I say, It's me.

Goddamnit, she says. You guys kill me.

But she shoves over in her bed and makes room for me, and I lie back next to her trying not to touch her too much. Her body is warm and a little damp.

It's The Ho, I say.

I know, she says. She lifts my arm and puts her head kind of in my armpit, kind of on my shoulder. She's so small. She's half the size of me. I stay with her while she cries and I want her and I know she's begging me, but The Ho's my friend.

So The Ho goes to juvey for six months. And the rest of us get jobs at McDonald's and Dunkin' Donuts and try to forget it could be worse.

On The Ho's eighteenth birthday, he's finally up for parole. We drag our sorry asses to Detroit to watch him stand in the courtroom, put his hand over his heart, and tell the judge he plans to serve this great country of ours in this great war for democracy if they let him off without a tether.

I sit on the hard, slick bench with Rochelle, who smells like lilac bushes in the spring and hairspray and frosted cinnamon roll. She clutches my arm.

Don't worry, I whisper into her sticky curls.

I know The Ho's lying. Of course he'll come home to her and to us, too, nights playing Grand Theft Auto and TrickSkate after his dad's passed out on the couch.

But the mess of it is that Little Ho actually signs up. Enlists.

I dare you, or I would dare you if I could, to ask The Ho to define democracy. I don't think he'd have any more idea than Richie. But The Ho has to put on a good show, has to take the risk the rest of us never would. He's still trying to make up for what happened when he and Ball were in juvey for robbing the Hungry Howie's with a BB gun, of all things. One of those juvey guys got Little Ho good in the shower. That's what Ball says, anyway. And of course, there is what happened later, too, which I know is true because I was there. But I've always got The Ho's back, and I say what he says: he got his nickname from the ladies. And some people believe him, too, and say he's no faggot. But when in doubt, nothing's as good a show here in Deep as prepping to blow up Iraqi balls.

So we're standing outside one night in February on the front porch of his dad's trailer freezing our asses off for a smoke when he tells me the news, that the fake plan has turned into his real gig.

No shit? I ask, feeling my gut clench, but I stay cool. Why?

Tether or no tether, he says, This is my life, Chuchie. He points with the two fingers that hug his Salem at the view of the interstate, the junk in the yard, the yellow light coming from the window of the trailer.

What about that G.E.D. course? I ask.

I ain't the smart one, Chuchie. That's you, he says.

What about our trip?

I can see the outline of his mouth as he bites his lower lip. We can do it when I get back, he says. It's only a couple of years.

We both know he has no choice. Even McDonald's won't hire a guy straight out of juvey, especially a guy who went in for holding steel. Who knows if the Marines will even take him.

But they do.

The Ho, he's got twenty-twenty vision, he's fast, he's small but strong. The recruiter practically jizzes all over him when he comes by to have him sign.

The Ho's dad, of course, doesn't even get off the couch when The Ho mentions he's signed, he's headed to boot camp. I'm there, and I see The Ho's dad, without taking his eyes off the game he's watching, wave one arm. And that's it.

That spring before The Ho leaves goes by fast because we're all broke and we've got to try for better jobs. I go for my G.E.D. and I put in at GM despite hearing nobody's getting in these days. And after I've boiled 20,000 frozen fries in oil and mopped a few hundred dozen floors, it's the day before The Ho goes and I've barely seen him. Maybe I've been avoiding him. Maybe it's because of Rochelle, but it seems like more than that, because I generally behave myself with her at this point, no matter what she says she wants.

So I drop by The Ho's place on my way home from work.

His father's still at the television, like he's never left it, and I don't see The Ho.

Where's Tom?

His father points to the bathroom.

You in there? I yell.

Doin' my head, he says. Wanna do it before I get there.

For some reason I'm nervous. I try to watch *Challenge of the Gladiators* but I can't sit still. I get up, walk into the bathroom. He's got half his head shaved, a mess of gold like the tassel on corn all over the floor.

You're a wreck, I say.

He hands me the clippers and I run them over his head until it's smooth. He turns to face me, holding in his bottom lip. I can tell I should touch him, but I don't know how. So I tell him I have to go home and have dinner with my grandma.

Of course, everyone's car happens to be shot that week, so we borrow a car, all on the ups this time, and we see Little Ho off at the airport.

When he stands there on the curb at Detroit Metro, he looks as small as Rochelle, who just clasps her arms over her ribs and stares at the sky the whole time, blinking the tears out of her mascara. It's warm but Rochelle is shivering, and Little Ho gives her the grey hooded sweatshirt he wears all the time so the ends of the sleeves are all ragged. He disappears through the glass doors and he doesn't look back.

So the rest of us wait through the three months of The Ho's boot camp. We keep our crap jobs and hone our crap habits. I see Rochelle Sundays while my grandma is at church, but mostly we just kiss until I wreck myself without even taking my pants off. I tell her I can't with her. I shouldn't. She says she's never even done it with The Ho and she's waiting for him, anyway. But she's just so lonely. The Ho writes her letters, but she never reads them to me. I ask if The Ho's okay. She says he misses her. I say I'm not jealous. We lay on the bed holding hands and passing a joint.

But when the others are there, say, sitting in Rochelle's mother's house and talking rot in general, we laugh at The Ho.

Every so often when Rochelle leaves the room to get us more beer, someone'll ask, Hey, how much you think he's taking it up the ass?

And everyone'll crack up.

I laugh because you can't not. But it catches in my throat, and Ball sees my face and for once in his life has a smart thought and takes me out to buy cigarettes. We get into Rochelle's car and head toward the gas station in town.

Ball knows it's his fault, I think, that shit that went down the first time The Ho got out of juvey. I barely knew him then. He was just some faggot from school. Anyway a group of older guys got wind of Ball's story about the shower and they decide to catch The Ho on his way out of the Wal-Mart where Rochelle works. They take him to the old cornfield out back of the building. Circle him. I don't know why, but Ball calls my grandma's house and tells me what's going down just in time for me to ride my bike over, just in time to see the slime who used to sell us weed walk up to the Ho with his hand on his crotch.

Let's see your action, faggot.

Worse thing I've ever seen. Those assholes start passing The Ho between them and Ball is cheering. They make a regular crop circle around him. And the thing is that the slime keeps beating Little Ho long after it's normal to stop. Once Ball gets bored and he's going to be late for getting Richie from work and heads out, the slime and his friends push The Ho face down.

You want to be a faggot huh? Huh?

I just stand there and watch, though I can't remember later exactly what it was like. Those three bastards take turns topping The Ho. I want to stop them but I don't know how without taking it up the ass myself. And since I'm still standing around when they're done and they're lighting their smokes, the slime says to me, *What, you want in on that action?*

And I don't have to answer because right then The Ho stands up. I see that he's one tough motherfucker. He puts out his hand to shake the slime's hand, which makes those bastards disappear real quick, and I have to go with them. You can't stay alone with a faggot.

I start my bike. But I hear The Ho puking as they walk away.

And for what reason I'll never know, I get worried that The Ho will die out there in that field. So once I get to the parking lot I tell those bastards I need smokes. I double back toward the Wal-Mart. I head back out through the broken-sharp corn. I offer The Ho a ride home.

Fuck you, he says, standing in the center of that circle they made.

Seriously, man, I say, putting my hand out to touch his arm.

I don't know why it matters so much, but I convince him to

get on the back of my bike. He wraps his arms around my waist, and I rev and ride extra fast over the rise of the back road that leads to the interstate, to The Ho's trailer. I ride by sometimes even now, but it's hard to remember that first night as much as I want to, the way The Ho came out of the shower with a dingy towel around his hips and heated up TV dinners in the microwave and opened my beer on the edge of the counter. I decide right then The Ho is decent people, and we'll get with him and make sure no one fucks with him again. And that's what bothers me when he leaves for the Marines. I'm breaking my own goddamned word.

And maybe Ball knows that's what I'm thinking in the car after he's rescued me from hanging out with our friends who don't know what they're laughing at. Crushed corn and blood. I'm the one on a goddamned tether. I'm the one that got us into The Ho, the one who made friends with the faggot. And Ball gets that you have to follow through on a thing like that, just like he follows through with Richie. But Ball doesn't say anything. He's nervous. He turns up the air conditioning until I can't breathe without hurting my lungs. He turns onto the main road.

Rochelle don't know a thing, Ball says at last.

Ball's just trying to be cool because not only is he a loser like the rest of us, but he takes home the donuts no one buys and eats them in front of porn. That's what Richie told me, and Richie's too dumb to make this kind of shit up.

She's got no idea her man's a swank, Ball tries again.

I want to kick his fat ass, but instead I tell him I don't want to talk about The Ho. It's too depressing.

I go into the gas station. It's hotter than hell in there. It's like I can't find any place to be comfortable. And instead of Marlboros I buy Salems like The Ho would. In the car I light two, passing one to Ball.

You think he'll make it through The Crucible? Ball asks, squinching up his eyes because he hates menthol. He backs out of the parking space, his gut pressing up against the wheel.

I think of Little Ho trying to walk for fifty hours with drill sergeants screaming in his face. Maybe it's raining on Parris Island or maybe he's sweating his balls off. Maybe someone is fucking The Ho.

Maybe he's happy and maybe he's hurting and maybe he'll know too much when he comes back. I guess it's hard to be a faggot anywhere.

He probably didn't make it, Ball goes on. He's probably packing his bags and ready to come home and get on welfare and make babies with Rochelle.

Shut the fuck up, Ball, or I'll kick your fat ass, I say at last.

Jesus, Chuchie. You need to get laid, he says, even though we all know that Ball's only gotten laid once, and it was the time we all got laid together in this old shed out back of Richie's by this girl Heather and that was way back in seventh grade.

Maybe I do need to get laid. In fact, I know I do, but I'd be an asshole if I knocked Rochelle despite the number of times she's dripped on me right through her skirt after we've macked for three hours. I've learned to live with blue balls permanently, I guess. You can't blame her. She'd let me if I'd do it.

I tell Ball I feel like shit and he drops me off at home where I lay back on my bed and point the fan on myself and smoke the entire fucking pack of smokes and think about the two guys in that book I stole heading for the ranch, making camp in the dark, talking their dreams. That was the thing The Ho and I got into that first night. This talk about riding my bike out to New Mexico somewhere. The Grand Freaking Canyon. *The fat of the land.* And I curl up on my side with the pillow over my head. It smells like Rochelle's hair. And maybe, I think, The Ho and I really could ride the bike across the country, and I fall asleep thinking that.

So that August The Ho gets ten days vacation between boot camp and more training, and we all ride together to pick him up at the airport. We stand waiting at the bottom of the stairs, and when we see him, it's like he's a ghost. It's like I know in advance that they're going to send Little Ho to Iraq first chance they get.

And they do.

So those ten days are the last days of our lives. We almost knock The Ho over running into him so hard, and he lifts Rochelle and they kiss and Richie lifts both of them and bounces so that Ball and I have to convince him to put them down before he shakes their brains out on the floor. Ball reaches around and pats The Ho on the back, and vice versa. The Ho looks at me. His eyes are tired and his skin is grey.

How's it goin', Chuchie?

I smile. It sucks, man, I say. I grab him around the neck and headlock him and rub the sandpaper of his scalp. I see the red skin, the long scar still trying to heal.

Let's get some chow, The Ho says.

And we head back to Rochelle's house, and hardly a one of us leaves for anything unless we have to. We play video games and watch movies and Rochelle's mom makes us burritos and buys us fresh beer. It's the end of summer, dry as bone, and we lay out on her back lawn on blankets until dawn. Ball and Richie are under one blanket and The Ho and Rochelle are under another and I am in the middle, on the dead grass. The Ho is between me and Rochelle, which should feel weird, you know, with all her rubbing up against me in those months he was gone, but it doesn't. It's like he's our kid or something.

We listen to the whisper of corn and no one needs to say much. We fall asleep and wake with the sun in our faces. Ball keeps us in donuts for breakfast. I keep us in burgers. And the days pass like that until ten are gone.

On the last night we just play hide-and-seek between the rows for hours like we're twelve or something. Ball is easy to find because the corn moves every which way when he so much as takes a step. And Richie's a mouth-breather. But it takes me a long time to find The Ho because now he knows how to hide. He knows how to sneak up and pounce on you without making a sound. He nails me a couple of times good. And I mean to get him back for it, but the next time I find him he's with Rochelle. He's holding her, her back pressed to his chest, her knees to her chin, her face streaming with black tears. I stay where I am. I watch.

And that night we get into more than beer. After everyone's gone to sleep and I think he has, too, I hear him stand up and walk away. I think he's just taking a piss, but he's gone for twenty minutes. I follow him into the corn and find him half-naked, wandering drunk in that field, his arms open to the sky. I let him sit with his back pressed to my chest. I don't know what to say, so I don't say anything. I hook my arm around his shoulders and pull his head back under my chin.

Josie Sigler

I feel him swallow. I smell the top of his head, a smell almost like bacon-grease mixed with peppermint. I inhale like I'm underwater, like smelling him will choke me. And he tells me the story no one wants to hear, the hazing, the shit smeared on his face, the butt of the rifle to his head.

He holds up his fingers in a peace sign. Semper Fi, he says. He laughs, his breath thick with whiskey. Then he nearly whispers, I asked her to marry me, Chuch.

What'd she say?

Yeah, he says. She said yeah.

And he goes back for Infantry within twenty-four hours and by the next spring he's deployed. Fallujah. Al Anbar. Iraq.

That fall I get into GM and everyone forgets that I was going to be a lawyer and Rochelle is moved up to manager and everyone forgets she was going to be a nurse. Ball is still at Dunkin' Donuts, and miracle of miracles, Richie is kicking the pants off all of us working for some mechanic in Rochester Hills, making enough money to get any girl he wants. Richie's good looking and hung like a donkey, too. He's always gonna score if he just keeps his mouth shut. Except, these chicks take his money all the time, and that's where I am when I find out—I'm in freaking Rochester Hills, arguing with some chick on Richie's behalf, and Ball shows up.

Fuck, man, fuck, is all he'll say for the first twenty minutes. And after he sits his fat ass down on the pavement, he says, The Ho.

And I know he's dead. I know Tom is dead.

But it's worse than that. He's been hurt. He called Rochelle from a hospital in Germany, where they transferred him after Operation Phantom Fury, whatever the fuck that's supposed to mean. Rochelle went over to Dunkin' Donuts and fell apart all over Ball. All I can hear is her voice, her pleading, coming through in Ball's voice when he looks up, tears bright in his eyes and says, They burned him, Chuchie. They burned him. I can see in his eyes Rochelle's brown and begging like a dog's for it to be untrue. I stare at the scuttling leaves and smell the first November snow in the air.

Not He got burned.

But They burned him, Chuchie.

So I walk away from Richie and Ball and the buck-toothed bitch fucking with Richie who's just been standing there listening to this shit and I hop on my bike and go to Rochelle's. I ride fast as I can over the rises and I try not to puke.

Rochelle is lying on her mother's couch. She's staring at the one picture he's sent, but in it you can't even see his face because the sun is behind him. He's pointing at the camera.

Later he'll tell us his story, the shake and bake, the white phosphorus fired into the trench lines, the spider holes, the smoke screen spreading, the screaming of women and children whose faces melted away. Things I can picture the edges of, but never really see. One kid whose whole body turns to ash. And when The Ho turns around, he doesn't see anyone else. He's covered from head to toe in gear and it's heavy and he's running out of oxygen. And then he feels like the devil himself has stabbed him in the crease between his left leg and his nuts. He's on fire but he can't see the fire. He wonders how he fucked up. He knows the only thing that will stop the burn is mud, and he throws himself down, and he waits and prays to die because the shit is eating away at his balls right up into his ass and bladder.

Rochelle raises her arms to me, letting The Ho flutter to the ground, and she says, Please.

We both cry the whole time. I'm bawling like a fag myself against her neck and I can't come. She's clawing at my back and biting my chest, banging her head against it, the tears mixing with the sweat in my hair. When we finally give up, when we lie there with our skins pressed together, she says, He took the hit for you. He did it for you, Chuchie. Because you ain't no loser.

I look down at The Ho's face in that photo on the floor and I see him pointing at me. I get up and pull my stinking T-shirt over the goose bumps.

I stop on my way out the door because I catch sight of The Ho's old hoodie hanging off the banister. And then all I can see is the moment we got to Caseville Beach that day, the way Little Ho ran straight to the water, stripping the hoodie off. I see his head disappearing in the waves and I see him come up laughing and myself running in after him and my arms around him as I hold him under and the drops on his

Josie Sigler

skin as he comes back up, wallops me on the back.

The Ho flies in from Germany a couple weeks later. This time his father picks him up at the airport because none of us can go. We've all got to work. And that night it's snowing like mad but I convince my grandma to let me have her car and I pick Rochelle up and we head over.

There's a white Corolla parked in the driveway, a car we've never seen.

We come in the door and see a woman in a nurse's uniform standing over The Ho, easing him from his wheelchair onto the couch, which is wrapped in a white sheet. She's juggling the tubes that lead to bags hanging off his chair. We see the bandages, the red and angry skin peeking out, the cave that shit made in his leg and gut. The Ho is pale and his eyes are rimmed in red as he stares at us, almost like he doesn't see us at all. The nurse looks over her shoulder at us.

I clear my throat. We're his friends, I explain.

Well, she says brightly, holding up a roll of gauze. You all just hold on a sec.

So we go out to the porch for a smoke.

You can never tell him, I say.

Rochelle nods, exhaling from her nostrils, closing her eyes. She keeps nodding.

Once the nurse leaves, we go back in the house and now The Ho is sitting on the couch with a blanket over his lap. He's watching TV and he reaches out with the remote and turns it way down, so we can just see the faces on the news, the new guys who'll head out to Baghdad, who have no idea what they're running from or to or who they'll be in less than two years.

What's up, you guys? he says, trying to sound like it's a regular Friday night.

Rochelle walks around his wheelchair to get to him but I stand in the doorway listening to his father's snores coming from the bedroom. She wraps her arms around his shoulders, awkward because he can't turn his body, and he doesn't hold her back, just leans his head, the hair already starting to grow out, on hers, which still shines with drops of melting snow. They sit like that and I lean in the doorway for what seems like an hour. I can't stop staring at the bag of yellow fluid hanging from the pole on his chair, and the darker bag wrapped in a towel beneath that.

I don't have to know yet the year that will follow, that The Ho will swallow his meds ten times a day and go crazy, that he'll tell me what it was like in the barracks, how he can't remember it or forget it. He'll beg me to take that Magnum that started all this trouble and kill him. I'll want to, and I'll dream of crop circles, of all the ways I should have saved him and didn't.

Do it, Chuchie, he'll say. And all I will say is he'll get better, we'll buy leather jackets and ride out to New Mexico. We'll go somewhere no one knows us and start over.

I'm a coward. I'm standing there in the doorway and I don't have to know the morning he'll wake up, drag himself from the couch to his father's bedside drawer, put that gun in his mouth, and do it himself. Rochelle coming in with a paper bag of groceries that she drops on the floor. Her mouth open in what looks like a scream but there'll be no noise, no tears.

And that night we first see The Ho, the way he's been returned to us, we just stare at the TV awhile without listening to it.

The Ho finally sends Rochelle into the kitchen to grab his meds and a can of beer for each of us. Once she's gone he looks at me and says, How you been?

I got in at GM, I say.

I know, he says.

Want to play Grand Theft Auto?

Sure.

MY LAST HORSE
[*Mustang*]

I heal horses. It isn't the world's most prosperous career, but I love it. And I'm good at it, despite the fact that I'm a woman and on the wiry side. No part of the job scares me—not the panicked eyes, the wolfish cough and whinny, the convulsions. I admit that I sometimes lack the good judgment older healers possess, but in this life courage counts. My mother, with whom I still speak on occasion despite my vows to eschew the outside world, says the difference between stupidity and courage is slim and can only be decided upon outcome, which depends on wind direction and star positions, too.

Mostly, I've been brave. At least where horses were concerned.

Marin, my mentor, founder of The Free Horse Ranch, let me go it alone for the first time when I was just twenty-two. A girl, really. Saving a horse a practiced healer could lose, beautiful palomino, horse of emperors and conquistadors. Her tongue hung between her lips like a man's tie, purple, as she choked. She thrashed, tossing her mane.

Of course, Marin said calmly, one thumb looped in his jeans, his other hand on the horse's wide back as she staggered between us, The only real power is that of choice. You get this horse to choose life, to accept no other solution, and she'll live, Edie.

Now, unlike my mother, I'm not a nervous person. I don't make predictions about the darkness of days to come. I don't pray. But it seemed this horse had been handed a no-win situation. Bad enough to make a heathen like me glance at the sky. My knees shook, threatened to give out. Marin stepped back, closed the gate behind him.

I took a breath out of that wide, wide blue and let the energy, my gift, swirl above me. Through me. I rested one hand at the base of the horse's pulsing neck, looked into the dark-rimmed eyes. My forehead opened gently and invisibly unto her forehead. I entered her mouth, pushing fearlessly past the back of the tongue and into the gullet to remove what had gathered dangerously there. My first horse closed her eyes, shuddered. Her throat seized on my wrist and her knees buckled. I tugged gently but firmly. I commanded the horse bone, the horse blood:

Rescue this whole horse. Let this horse live.

Chip and Jesse, two of the best horse hands I've ever known, clutched at the fence. They knew how much I wanted to move up, be recognized, be asked to stay at Free Horse for keeps. Come on, Edie, Chip whispered, ready to leap to my assistance should the horse's weight begin to fall toward me. Jesse took off his hat, wiped his face with a hanky. Marin's thin form leaned against the fence, nonchalant.

With a bit of dare in my veins and a final fruitful yank, I tossed the dark tarry mass to the mud. Horse-wound and earth steamed together. A yeasty tang rose from their union and stung my nostrils. My horse collapsed into the mud and weeping rose within me for the first time since my father died. I sank down, too, leaning my fatigued body into the massive ribcage of my first horse.

Then, softly at first, I felt from within her body a deep thumping, the rhythm of life jump-started. I turned to see her tongue begin to pink up. Struggling, she nonetheless stood, opened her eyes, looked past the green-yellow hills to the chokecherry trees, and then beyond the trees, past where the hands and healers go. My horse wanted to run. I wiped my slick palms on my jeans and kissed the soft place between her nostrils. I let go her mane. She ran, her back strong and shining like melted gold.

In the seconds before the darkness came, I knew I had been born.

Marin, vaulting the gate, caught me beneath the arms as I fell to the ground. My head ached. I could not see. Healing that horse had blinded me.

Don't worry, Marin said. It'll come back. It always does.

I lay in Marin's arms while my vision returned. When it did, his head blocked out the sun, white hair a swirling halo in the breeze, face deep with weather, eyes shimmering as lake, full of pride.

He said, slowly, quietly, double-checking: So you will stay here, then, with us at The Ranch?

I nodded, too tired to speak.

He began, I am afraid that you'll regret—

I know what you're worried about, Marin, I said, forcing myself to sit up.

Many of those lost to The Ranch are lost to cowardice and fear of living so far off the grid. But mostly, we lose folks to loneliness. To work with horses who've been abandoned, starved, poisoned—acts unmentionable in polite company—you must be a highly trained horse-hand or in a tenth of a percent of profoundly intuitive born healers, like me. You must exist for the horses, not riches or recognition or even thanks. You don't have time for flossing, let alone love.

Still, on occasion, Chip, Jesse, or one of the others brought a woman home from a weekend spent carousing. She'd fall in love with the man, the land, and the mission, in that order. But it's hard on a woman to live for man alone. Bored or exhausted by playing second fiddle to horses squalling in the night, women get restless. They leave after a few months, despite the earth here that smells like a wild mushroom, the air that presses into your skin like a body, the hills. When a woman leaves, many a man follows, claiming true love. Love, nothing. As a man begins to understand the true sacrifices he must make to live the life he dreams of, he often loses his courage for such a life.

You don't have to worry about that with me, Marin. I know what I want. I do.

I wanted to stay. I wanted to be something. I wanted to heal horses. I wanted it more than I had ever wanted anything.

Until I met Janice.

My mother used to say and I never believed her: Edie, the Lord doesn't load up one plate but He loads up a second. Leaves you hungry choosing which plate to eat off of. Growing up, I was always hungry, and figured quietly to myself that I'd just eat off both plates if such a thing happened to me. I guess that's what I did with Janice and the horses. But of course, I never thought it was God who sent me to heal horses or to find Janice. It was Marin.

I had been at The Ranch over a year, healing horses diligently. I hadn't visited my mother in months, nor had I left for any frivolous reason. Thus, one morning at breakfast Marin put down his paper, looked over his spectacles and said, You know, you should get out for a night every now and then. You like jazz? You like country? This lady who's opening at The Red Wheel—I saw her act once in Topshamie—she's got a voice could make caramel . . . melt glass. . . .

So I cleaned up at the washtub and borrowed Marin's old Mustang. I drove a hundred miles to sit in the only bar in Dianville and listen to Janice sing.

I ordered a beer and milled through the considerable crowd to find a table in front. If you're going to do something, do it fully, I say. Sit in front. It was so loud that when Janice first came through the haze of cigarette smoke and grease seeping from batter-fried food to leave sour ghosts in the air, no one paid much attention. Except me. I was close enough to touch the long molten-orangey braid that swung out from behind her shoulder as she settled onto her stool. She brushed her cheek against her white-shirted shoulder and grabbed the neck of her guitar.

This, too, was like the moment you get born.

Janice tuned up, tapped her foot. She hummed into the microphone. The patrons went on eating, playing cards. Some glanced up when Janice strummed a few chords. When she shoved the microphone away, stood, and let out a note that was wider than any horizon, high and low mixed together throbbing, forks clattered on plates. Housewives cried into their french fries, I swear. Janice's throat vibrated so that the skin there shimmered like the air during corn spell. Her voice was as open as a foaling horse and aching just as much. But in that moment, for the first time in a long time, I did not think of horses. All I knew right then was that I had to meet Janice.

After an hour of everything from Wynette to Holiday, she left the stage amid an uproar of applause. The folks in Dianville, while accustomed to a deeply moving tractor-pull now and then, had not seen the likes of Janice. They surrounded her.

When the crowd cooled and the manager handed Janice a beer, I stood up, shake-kneed, and headed over.

Hey, Janice said, a lilt in her tone, a slight hoarseness. Tendrils of red hair stood out at her temples.

I replied, quite brilliantly, Your voice. Your voice.

She laughed, her eyes turning half-moons above her freckled cheeks. Freckles like stars.

I'm here for the summer, she said, pointing to a flyer that hung over the bathroom.

I was never the kind of person to go after just anything, you understand. But every chance I got that spring I slicked my hair, put on jeans unsmudged by horse flop and etcetera, and pointed Marin's old 'Stang toward Dianville. I stayed until closing. I pretended to be interested in drinking, often rendering myself unable to drive home. I can't tell you how many nights I slept in the backseat with the top down, staring up at the stars, happy as a clam. I arrived back home mornings amid hoots from Chip, Jesse, and the guys. I had a hell of headache half of the time. But it paid off. Janice began to expect me. She smiled when she saw me come in. Soon it seemed she was singing right to me, only to me, in answer to an unspoken question.

I didn't even know exactly what I was asking for. But Janice did.

One night, as I prepared to shuffle out, she walked over, caught my hand. The bones of her fingers were like loose bullets covered with velvet and calloused at the tips. They sent a shock up my arm, a new electricity.

Why don't you just stay awhile, have another beer?

She led me to the bar, which the bartender wiped even as he rolled his eyes.

Gimme two Coronas, she said.

We went out back to the alley where a sweaty mist clung to dumpsters. We sat on the hood of an old Buick missing its front wheels. Janice's voice floated like fried-honey all over brick and cool alleyway air in the dark. She had been on the road for five years, playing the small towns. She dreamed of making it to Nashville. Nashville was where it was at. As soon as she made enough money she would move onto the next gig, and the next, until she got there.

So what do you do? she asked, blowing the smoke from her Winston over her shoulder.

I was still at the beginning of my career, a career without benefits or awards or ceremonies, a career full of spit and blood, not sequins and songs.

I heal horses, I said.

She leaned back, stared a long moment before she said, So, you got the touch.

The horses and I get each other, I said, feeling the blood rush into my cheeks.

Janice said that she could remember a time when she spoke with horses, when everyone did. That's why all seven-year-old girls dream of horses, she sighed, twirling the end of her long red braid around her finger, because they can still understand the language.

Up close, Janice's eyes were like the earth in the moment it suddenly turns toward spring. She took a long pull on her beer. I had never wanted to be the rim of a bottle so badly before. She offered me a sip. The sweltering air wound around our legs propped on the bumper, but she had goose bumps. We scooted closer to each other. I felt her bare thigh press against mine in jeans. Her hand slid up my arm. Then, as simply as a horse takes half an apple from your palm, Janice's soft mouth covered mine.

In that moment, I forgot horses existed. Well, almost.

Later that week Marin said, Be careful. Yours is not the average life.

Janice knows that, I told him.

After all, deep within Janice, too, an essential energy rose and crested when she sang. The more I saw of her, the stronger I felt. In fact, any talents I may have had only presented themselves more fiercely. Every horse I got, no matter what she had suffered, found comfort in my hands.

Marin reminded me that we can't take too much credit for our talents without thanking the wounds that engendered them.

The winter my father died, I was twelve. Even as the months passed, I still felt him standing in doorways. I ached so it seemed a beehive had grown in my throat. My mother touched my forehead and said that while hurt surely comes in with her knife, she bears a basket of jellies, too.

I say be wary when someone gives you a gift too sweet.

Come home with me, Janice said, finally, one night after we'd slid around on the hood of that old Buick for two hours or more.

I don't like to leave the horses overnight, I said.

I waited in the parking lot of her motel while she packed. I caught her in my arms when she came running down the stairs, falling over with the weight of her two carpetbaggy suitcases and her guitar. I still remember the way she slung that Martin over her shoulder easily, as if it were a piece of her body. The way she got in the car and crossed her slender ankles.

Of course, the guys gave me hell at first. But Janice, unlike the other women who had visited here, found her niche. Once she took over the kitchen, no one complained or teased again. We all began to rise a bit earlier to be first in line for biscuits sopped in Janice's thick, rich gravy, eggs with lacy white edges. And in the evenings, if we didn't go to Dianville, we joined the others around the fire. When her voice rose strong and high and brazen above all of ours, above the smoke and fireflies, who could've failed to love her? Chip and Jesse stared with envy at her hand, illuminated by fire, squeezing my shoulder.

On the back porch of The Red Wheel early that autumn, Janice told me her gig had been extended. Normally, she said, she'd have turned that down, moved on. But. . . . She looked so deeply into my eyes that I felt she saw everything, saw all the way to the soles of my feet, saw my pimpled face at thirteen years old and my first colicky wails. I hate to admit it scared me.

We built a modest cabin at the far edge of the land in the rising mist that tucked us away. Having survived a frigid winter during which we were forced to sleep some nights in the stable, warmed by the breath of mending horses, I wanted to get the new place roofed and sealed before the snow flew. One Friday in October, as I was pounding nails into shingles, Janice yelled up to me, Babe, time to go!

I climbed down the ladder. I can't tonight, I said. I have to get this squared away.

When Janice got home that night, she climbed into bed without saying a word.

In the morning, I apologized. But she said nothing. I felt like a fool in front of the guys at breakfast when Janice would not answer the most basic question I asked.

Uh-oh, Edie's in trouble with her gal, teased Chip, shaming me with one finger against the other like he was grating a carrot.

Nothing a night off can't fix, I said, forcing a laugh.

I still don't know why, but the more Janice wanted me to go with her, the more I wanted to stay home. And the more I refused to go, the more important my presence became. When Janice left for weekend gigs, I was a miserable wreck. I sat on my front porch chair and drank whiskey and stared in our window.

Lying in my arms late one night, Janice said, simply, Come with me to Nashville.

The horses, I said.

She begged me.

You'll have to choose, I said.

Please, she said.

It's your decision, I said.

And so I came in from a long day of healing horses to find all of her gone. Even her hairbrush with its tangles of fire.

That particular winter was mild in the North Country, but we had a run with some horses no one could convince of life's merits. I saw three horses put down in three weeks. The last was one of ours, Tiranthe, a good horse, who died with her head in my lap, her mouth throwing desperate whip-clouds into the chilled air until the last second. I was in the room when my father died. But even the details of his death have not stayed with me like the wild eyes of that horse.

My first dry spell, and I did not know that dry spells passed.

Spring is welcome most anywhere, but with the crocuses that year came the hope I needed. Nights brought a sweet smell down from the tall red trees as they grew their buds. I no longer woke with a dripping nose, sore fingers. I washed at the creek's bubbling edge. A soft pain was in the air, a want I could not identify. And one morning it led me to get in the car and drive. And you know where I ended up. My hand on the valley between Janice's shoulder blades as she sat on the bed, her knees bent, her feet on the floor of her motel room.

Things gotta change, Edie, she said.

Anything, I said.

But after hours of the kind of talking that only lovers can do, the kind that makes you feel as if your very life force is seeping through your forehead, I could not help but repeat again and again that the only solution was for her to quit. Her work was causing too much friction. She had never meant to be a regular at the Wheel, the commute was long, the job did not pay much, it distracted her from her work at The Ranch, which was essential. We had to eat.

I guess it's only reasonable, Janice said. I can't keep working two jobs forever.

What about the other gigs? The travel?

I'll have to adjust, she said. It's too much to be apart like that. We gotta grow up someday, she said, sounding an awful lot like my mother when I complained of my first job, mucking out stalls. A job's a job, right? It's about having clothes on your back and food on the table. Unless, of course, it was my job. My job was just too important. My job provided us a home. My job was our family. Janice agreed. Besides, she said, Being here's the first time in my life I got a chance to be still. I always wanted to try a quiet life. What can you do but believe what people say?

Except, my mother always says you have to listen to people's eyes, too, if you want the true story. In second grade, a teacher had shown a picture from the *National Geographic*, a close-up of a tiger's face just as she caught and crushed the hind leg of an antelope with her powerful jaws. It wasn't that face I stared at, but the eye of the antelope, off-center, down in the photograph's corner, as it accepted its fate. I registered Janice's suffering as similar, but a tiger does what it does until it dies. A tiger does not see what an antelope sees, or it would cease being a tiger.

But you must keep balance, Edie! Marin said, gently fingering a laceration on the bulged jaw of a sleeping stallion. Janice had a whole life before you.

I know Marin. But people change, I said, handing him the salve.

Do they? he said mildly, raising his eyebrows quickly at me before he plunged his finger, sticky with salve, deftly into the stallion's flesh. The horse, even in his sleep, jumped, threw his muscled neck back and away from the healing finger.

I bent to stroke the clotted mane. They do, I assured him.

If our life together was any evidence, Janice had surely given up her Nashville dreams, a fact for which I was glad—not because I wanted her to give up playing. In fact, I was the first to tell you how much I loved her songs. But music? It could be made anywhere. And Janice had grown to love the horses that visited the humble but wide space between the trees and the creek. She turned our mess-kitchen into a real kitchen. I'd pause in my work to look in the window and see her red braid tangled, brow furrowed, the front of her jeans covered with flour. God, I loved her, couldn't wait to strip off those mussed jeans, hear that glorious voice talking to me.

Evenings, in our tub perched on the back porch, flour and millet and horse hair and pollen danced together on the water's surface as we recounted the day. What was she thinking as she kneaded, drew our bath?

Not much, she said. There aren't too many things interesting to tell about pulling beets and baking bread.

I had to agree. We both preferred to talk about the day's healing projects, the horses saved, and, on rare occasion, the horses lost. I, of course, could elaborate upon this topic until the sun fell from the sky, reveling in my own genius if horses lived, despairing on the rare occasions they didn't.

We curled up on the porch even on the cool evenings, listening to the rapid pulse of hooves, the throbbing of the ground as the horses ran. We could see only the whitest horses running at the edge of the ranch. I showed Janice how you could tell, by the way the white horses moved, where the dark horses were, the chestnut, the black.

On an autumn night that marked our second anniversary I woke under a down blanket on the porch alone, a chill having sunk into my bones. I stood, stretched, and looked in the window.

Janice sat on the bed. Her guitar, which she had not touched in months, was in her lap. She held it lightly, stroking its waist as gently as she had stroked mine just hours before. She cradled it. Brought her forehead to its strings. Then, she put it in its case. I walked into the house, pretending I'd seen nothing.

The next afternoon, between one horse and another, I brought Janice's guitar to where she was shucking corn behind the mess-kitchen, and asked her to play.

I don't feel like it, she said.

Why?

She shrugged and looked away. I got work to do, Edie. Like the rest of you.

I quizzed her. Did she miss singing in front of a crowd bigger than me and the guys around the fire at night?

She sighed, brushing her hair from her face with her forearm, and, resigned, set down the ear of corn. Edie, she said, I've done what you asked. Now just let it be.

Later that day, when I stepped through the door to the mess-kitchen in search of a cold glass of lemonade, Janice was sitting across the table from Marin. Framed by the window, the two shone with incredible sadness. In Marin, such sorrow was organic, the burden of a healer, part of his posture. But Janice was bent forward against the rough grain as she wept. Marin's wrinkled hand awkwardly stroked her hair, as my father might have done to mine when I failed a spelling test or fought with my mother. Marin tipped his head toward the door, signaling that I should take my leave, which I did, not because I feel so compelled to do everything Marin suggests, but because I knew Janice needed to cool down. She always did.

My mother once said that bad blood left overnight wasn't fixable. The last thing I wanted was something broken for keeps between me and Marin, whom I admired more than anyone. I walked out into the yellow July dust toward his blue form bent fixing the rough-hewn fence. A pile of logs still glittered with sawdust lay stacked just beyond. We took refuge from the sun by sitting in their shadow, a private space to talk. I recited my usual to Marin. Janice was unreasonable. Janice asked for the impossible. I loved Janice, but she had to realize.

Marin said, I hate to say I told you so, but this is no kind of life for Janice. And eventually, if you keep her . . .

I haven't been *keeping* her.

Edie, he said, What makes a horse sick?

Come on, Marin. Janice isn't sick. Missing this trip isn't going to kill her.

Edie! Answer the question.

I rolled my eyes, but I answered. One time out of ten it's cruelty. Nine, it's passive. Somebody's left the horse out too long without feeding her. Forgotten about her. Or maybe given her something that Mother Nature wouldn't give her.

Ok. So, Janice's music is her feed.

I'm not keeping her from playing—

It doesn't matter. You don't have to cut her fingers off to stop her. All you have to do is make her feel like it doesn't matter to you. To cling to her if you know you're hurting—

I'm the one clinging? I said incredulously but evenly.

Marin reached out, touched my shoulder. Hey, he said, I'm not the enemy. I'm just saying that if you know what's happening to Janice and you contribute to it, then it's no longer just a mistake or circumstance, Edie. It's cruelty. You're a healer. It goes against everything you stand for.

I knew he was right. But I pressed on: What was the likelihood of her having made it, anyway? You know how many people go to Nashville thinking they're Loretta Lynn? Janice is not Loretta Lynn, because only Loretta Lynn is Loretta Lynn.

I heard a shuffling noise from the other side of the pile of logs. When I saw the look on Marin's face, it didn't take me long to realize that Janice was right behind me. But I did not look up. I kept my composure. I would deny what I'd said. I let a moment pass before I turned around to accept the basket of bread in her hand. Her lips were pale and tight. Her squinted eyes would not look at me, either.

That night, as if nothing had happened, I asked Janice to play. And like a robot, she rose from her chair, got her guitar, went to the porch, and played. And played. At first she played bits of songs I recognized, but soon they became a schizophrenic soup of words and rhythms, chords that sounded like an animal dying. She played after I had tired of listening.

I have to go to bed, I said, pretending her behavior was normal. On occasion, when you pretend a horse isn't sick, he ceases to be sick. I don't presume to understand this mystery, but I have seen it happen. I kissed Janice on her forehead, tasting her slight sweat. I repeated myself. Janice did not hear me. She went on in a kind of trance, her fingers strumming, her eyes closed.

When I woke in the morning, she was still sitting on the front porch, her face and hair making the flag of a country that did not exist. Her fingers were split and bleeding. I tried to take her guitar, which she clutched. I wrested it from her and set it aside, lifted her into my arms, and put her in the bed, covering her.

I went to the mess-kitchen to make bread, which, of course, was a disaster. Janice was practicing last night, I explained lamely to the guys.

Jesse, clueless, said, Dang, she plays a mean guitar when she wants to, don't she?

The mournful sound of the guitar haunted me all morning as we tried to save a starved Pinto, a young horse whose ribs pushed against her colored patches. We'd been forced to move her on a thick tarp because when a horse stays down too long she finds herself unable to walk. Although Chip and Jesse had gotten her onto the tarp, the ride to The Ranch had tired and frightened her. Each time one of us came near her, she reeled her head, panicking, trying to run on legs that just flopped uselessly in the air. There is little to be done for starvation except to offer nourishment. I could not use my hands, my heart, the light. When a horse is so hungry for so long, she no longer trusts the earth, let alone people.

We need to let her go, said Marin, heading to the barn to get the kit.

I looked down into the trough of water the horse would not drink. I saw my own thin face, my set jaw. No, I said.

What? Marin stopped in his tracks.

Let's keep trying. She just needs time.

Chip and Jesse made themselves scarce.

Marin strode back to me, standing as close to the dying horse as I could get, and took the flesh of my upper arm. He pushed my body toward the horse, who lurched in her wild attempts to flee from me. That's no way to live, Edie. No way to live.

We could try any number of—

Edie. We save horses for the horses, not for ourselves. You can go soak your head while I do what needs to be done, or you can give me a hand.

When the horse was still, I sat with her, patting the wasted muscles of her neck. I closed her eyes and lips and picked the grass from her lashes. Then I made dinner, which was no better than breakfast.

When I finally finished the dishes and returned to the cabin, Janice had bathed. She apologized to me, throwing her arms around my neck. I crawled in beside her, put my hand up her T-shirt and stroked the skin on her back. Every inch of Janice is as soft as the space between a horse's nostrils. Something you can't stop touching. She rolled over into me. I felt her tears on my collarbone. I said I was sorry. I repeated it over and over in the dark. I said it with each kiss. I was terrified of my own selfishness. I saw it flash up every connection our bodies made, like a constellation demanding its story be told. And, like a body of stars, it left at daybreak. As the sun rose, I held Janice in the crook of my arm. I would fix this. I vowed to pay her more attention. I promised more time around the fire. Maybe Janice could get her old gig at The Wheel. Or we could vacation to Nashville once I got a break. If she could not live there, at least we could visit.

But the next morning, a Rocky Mountain Horse with bone cancer, having snapped her femur, was brought in, and I forgot all about those plans. The horses, you see, were my family, my priority. Janice knew that.

That's love, she said, serving up a scone to Jesse. You make the sacrifice.

Jesse nodded and pounded his fist lightly on the table in a gesture of approval.

Chip said, Yeah, well I'm sorry for your singing career, Jan, but what Edie does here is life or death. Life or death can't be messed with, y'know?

I know. Janice gave him a watery smile.

Marin looked up frowning, then, from the book he was reading.

Define life, he said, standing. He dropped the book onto the table, making a brown circle of coffee dance in each mug, and walked quietly out of the kitchen, throwing one more look my way. Define death. Define life.

Whew, said Jesse. Somebody got a bug up his shorts.

Janice put down the plate of scones, and walked from the room.

That night, I found her guitar at the foot of our steps, smashed, neck broken, just its strings holding it together. I wrapped its pieces in a burlap sack and tucked it behind an old pile of equipment in the barn.

This past April, Janice was tired a lot. I'd take her in my arms and before I knew it, she was asleep. Sometimes I lay holding her like that, thinking about the horses, watching their midnight dance.

One afternoon, I called her into the yard to have her test Mabel, an extremely skittish but lovely white horse I was whispering. She could not be tested by one of the guys, who were too heavy, too loud.

The day was uncharacteristically hot. The usual rain had not come and dust clouds shimmered on the horizon. The few horses that had come in from beyond the line of trees were nervous. The studs bucked and tore at the air with their hooves. When I called, Janice came running from the kitchen, her feet bare and caked with flour and what looked like egg. She wiped her hands on the back of her jeans.

What ya need? Her brow was furrowed.

Can you test Mabel?

Sure, Janice said, softening. Her upper lip was sweaty, something I've always found particularly endearing about her, the way three or four droplets can gather and cling above her anchor-shaped smile.

I boosted her up. That was when I saw the bruise. The color of beet juice on a white towel, it emerged from the bottom of her jeans. It took me a second to realize it was her ankle, her skin, that color.

What's that from? I asked.

Oh that, she said, twisting to look down. Not sure.

That night, I laid her on the bed and lifted her nightgown. Her legs were covered with bruises the size of my fist, like blood vessels were bombs detonating beneath her pale skin.

We left The Ranch the following day, together. Janice rested her hand in my lap as I drove. She sang along loudly to the radio so I could sing with her, my terrible tuneless voice masked by hers, although I could tell singing was an effort. The doctor in Dianville said we'd have to go to the city. The doctor in the city hospital confirmed easily what we had already guessed. Janice accepted the news calmly, and asked, simply, to go home.

I knelt before her. You want me to find tickets to your mother's? I asked.

No, she said. Home home.

So I took Janice back to The Free Horse Ranch, vowing to spend every last moment with her. As Janice struggled on, I thought back to all the times when I had considered myself courageous. I tried to believe that I merely did what I had to do. It's the mantra of many a coward.

Spring turned into summer. Janice's red hair fell out and littered the white sheets and wooden floors. Every piece I found, I collected and wrapped in a piece of paper, until folded squares littered the table. Each morning, I tied one of my bandanas over her head. My mother said once that pride was a powerful vitamin. It's true that you can win a horse's favor by appealing to his sense of self. This is why we groom them so carefully. I told Janice how beautiful she was.

When she could no longer speak much, I ached for her voice. We slept before the open window all summer. I tried to listen inside Janice, like I often do with horses, but to no avail. Once she held her finger to my lips, as if she could tell what I was doing.

Stop trying, she said. I held those words. It would be days before more came.

Leaves littered the ground the afternoon Chip came calling. I was sitting with Janice on our front porch, trying to feed her some broth from a spoon, but she could not swallow.

Horse come in, Chip said. You gotta take it. Dehydration, I think.

Bitterly, I said, Why can't Marin do it?

Go on, Janice rasped. It's your work. I kissed her on the end of her nose. I put on my hat and went in search of the horse.

But when I got to the stable, I could find no sign of a horse, just Jesse at the edge of the property, fussing with the car.

Jesse! I shouted.

He looked up.

Where's the horse? I asked.

He shook his head. No horse I know of. Marin said to work on this engine.

I stomped off before he could finish, headed to our cabin, stopped short by the sight of Marin and Chip kneeling before Janice. In Marin's hand was an enormous syringe. My gut went to ice.

No, I said. But I, too, knelt before Janice.

The men stood and walked away. Marin put his hand on my shoulder.

And there, on the porch on a cold autumn day, Janice took her last breath, which rattled out through that God-given voice box in a long whisper. Maybe Janice was saying she loved me, or she forgave me. But I hope she was singing.

I closed Janice's eyes and mouth. I carried her to our bed for the last time.

I found Marin and Chip behind the stable. Jesse was there, too, wide-eyed and dazed. I waited for the right words. They didn't come. I lunged forward and caught Marin around the waist, throwing him into the dust. I straddled him. Raising my fist, I smashed it down into his mouth. He didn't fight back. He just stared at me, pityingly. I raised my fist to hit him again, but Chip caught it. Jesse clasped my other arm. I lowered my head onto Marin's chest and wept. He stroked my head.

It was the best thing, Edie.

And I knew that, hard as it was to know. Especially for someone like me. My mother always said I was hard-headed. Even Janice, once, before she lost her voice, said that she knew, soon as we kissed, the course of events that would follow. The danger. That she understood the sacrifices she was making, and knew I could not make them. I only wish I was that smart, that I had known what I was giving up, what I would lose. I say that I heal horses, and I still think of myself as a horse-healer, but really, since Janice has been gone, the magic has left my hands. I eat supper with Marin and the guys. I teach. I tell every stud of a healer who struts onto this beautiful ranch without a clue about the real magic, the stuff you can't perform. The chances you get, the choices you make, only once in a lifetime.

This winter, I dug out Janice's guitar and polished each broken piece. Janice's family had buried her body, but I buried her, too, under a chokecherry tree that stands alone on a rise I can see from my window. The cold earth cradled and reclaimed the curved and ragged bits of that wood she most often touched. I unfolded every sheet of paper containing a red hair, put my hand into the wind and let go. Janice's hair danced briefly before me, then disappeared. On occasion, I find a strand pushed up against the rough wall of the barn or resting like a line of fire in snow. And some nights, out here in the North Country, when you're up late waiting for a horse or something else hurting, you'll hear this singing that some people say is the wind.

I know better.

CHICKEN
[Comet]

Chicken was stupid and dangerous, which should have been obvious, especially after Marlo vanished. But it's also the kind of game that hooks you right away. The first time you see it done, you go back to your apartment and eat dinner and sit around watching TV with your parents like nothing's changed. You go to bed like usual. Then you toss and turn, your skin burning while you think of strategies, almost against your will.

That night was foggy. Thick clouds moved over the highway and in the branches of the trees. Everything smelled of fallen leaves and the cigarette Marlo was smoking. He squinted at each set of headlights that appeared at the top of the hill. The other guys gathered around him on the road's shoulder, trying to be at least half as cool. But Marlo was sixteen and the rest of us were thirteen, fourteen.

I was the new kid. I came with Carter, the only guy I knew from my building. We had been messing around with the action-sensor lights in our complex's playground, seeing if we could snake-crawl on the gravel from one side to the other without tripping the sensor. We were both planning for the army. Just when I had him beat, he said he had to leave, it was almost time for Chicken. And boy was he gonna make a go of it tonight, give old Marlo a run for his money.

A go of what? I had asked.

Jesus, O'Cleary, he said, You are *such* a pussy.

You're the freakin' pussy, I said. So of course I had to follow him through the field outside the complex, had to take on whatever challenge was next. But the truth is, I *was* somewhat cautious by nature back then. I was standing there in the damp air worrying that my mom, on a late trip to the laundry room, would see darkness where she expected that safe circle of light, her son contained within it, his new little friend Carter.

Several cars passed: an Audi as stupid-looking as any, a Thunderbird, a Volvo station wagon about the size of my family's apartment, even a sweet old Monte Carlo. Marlo wrinkled his nose, shook his head at each. Too slow. Too easy. But his ears perked up to a rumble the rest of us heard, too. We turned together to look.

A huge brown UPS truck topped the hill at a decent pace and gained momentum as it came down. In the blink of an eye, Marlo tossed his cigarette to the ground, stepped on it, adjusted the collar of his jean jacket, and ran, graceful as a gazelle, into the road. The driver slammed on his brakes and the truck careened. Marlo's body, like a pencil in a glass of water, curved away from the truck, the light blue inside of his jacket briefly illuminated as it flapped open behind him. Then he disappeared. By the time the driver leaned on his horn, deafening the rest of us, Marlo was strolling on the median in the glow of the streetlight, flipping another cigarette into his lips.

Carter bent over and clutched his knees, shaking with laughter. He stood and popped at the air quick with each fist.

That Marlo's a dragon, he said, cackling. A bona fide freakin' dragon. He pointed his finger at the now-empty road. *That's* Chicken, he said.

I was shaking. Why? I asked. I couldn't help it.

Why did the chicken cross the road? Carter asked, and cracked up. Get it?

Sure, I said.

He grabbed me by the shoulder and said, To get to the other side. He got closer, stared right into my eyes. There's no point to any of it, he said. Gonna die when you're gonna die. So get your kicks while you can.

Carter stepped away from me and closed his eyes. He held out his arms as if crucified. Without further hesitation, he ran into the road just as a rusty old S-10 came barreling down. He tore crookedly toward the median where he tripped and rolled on the ground.

Jesus, I said, sounding like my mother, who always clutched at her neck when she heard any tragic tale: people being secret lovers, secret crackheads, secret flame-swallowers, whatever.

Yeah, said this smaller kid they called Prez because his real name was Roger Smith, like the CEO of GM. Carter's crazy. Yeah. Got a wicked death wish, that one.

Do you play? I said, trying to sound casual.

Sometimes, Prez said absently, looking away from me to watch the next runner, a lanky kid with a buzzcut and an old letterman jacket, approaching the road.

Every once in awhile, I do, Prez said, crossing his arms, his eyes on the hill. The runner hopped up and down, psyching himself up like he was at the Olympics.

I mostly watch, though, Prez said so quietly I could have missed it in the hoot and honk of Letterman darting into the road.

The kid was a zagger: instead of running all the way across, he stopped suddenly to avoid the boxy old Caddy speeding down the hill. It screeched away from him diagonally as he spun out into the tail lights. The driver of the Caddy put the flashers on, pulled onto the shoulder where we stood. The geezer opened the car door and tried to get out, but his seatbelt snapped him back into that fine leather bucket. Seconds later, he emerged bowlegged in his red polyester pants, shaking his fist, spewing a slew of curses and threats.

Game over, Prez said.

The others scattered. I stood watching Carter and Letterman running up the median. Where was Marlo?

Come on, Prez said to me. I looked past the median to the Southbound side. I caught what I thought was a glimpse of Marlo's slick but colorless hair through the window of another stopped car, a mid-70s puke-green Comet. I swear he was *inside* the car, though Letterman would argue later that he'd never gotten in, he'd simply disappeared, no shit, into thin air.

Prez pulled my arm. New Kid! he barked. We gotta bail. And

we ran way out into the field together, finally tossing ourselves down sweaty in the tall grass.

It was there, on the cold earth with Prez, that the first little buzzing came deep in my brain. I felt taller as I walked home, more like a man as I bent down to kiss my mother crocheting a blanket on the couch.

You're awful late, she said. I was worried sick.

I didn't respond. I merely clasped my hand on my dad's shoulder and he looked up from the TV, bleary-eyed. Yes, I felt a man. And I hadn't even been *it* yet. But that's the thing about Chicken. Even before you go, you've gone. Even if you sleep, a roadside figure hovers at the edge of your dream, waiting. When you come upon him, turn him around, you see he's you.

The next night my mom put up an enormous fuss, said I couldn't go to the playground, safety lights or no safety lights. I begged her, telling her this game I was playing with Carter wasn't like other games. This game was important for my future in the military.

Alright, she relented finally. But stay in the complex, and stay with Carter.

Of course, as soon as she let me go, I left the complex, headed for the highway. I tailed Carter at a distance most of the way, feeling this at least minimally met her requirements.

We waited, but Marlo never showed. I was so busy thinking about trying it all out, I had forgotten about the Comet. With each minute that passed, Letterman got more and more nervous.

It was UFO shit, he said. Marlo got beamed up.

I saw him get into a car, I said. It wasn't exactly true, but it felt true. Green Comet.

No, said Letterman. No way. I was closer, and I'm telling you, our boy downright evaporated.

Listen, I said. He was talking to the driver. I remembered the driver then: thin, white, forty-ish, mustache.

There was no Comet. I saw an old blue Maverick at some point, but no Comet. I think you're confusing the *idea* of a comet with the *name* of the car.

No way, I said.

Maybe he got hit, Prez tried, tentatively. Maybe he got sucked right under. But nobody listened to him.

Tell you what, Carter said, looking at me and then at Letterman. You're both full of shit. It's simple. Chicken went chickenshit, is all. It was bound to happen sooner or later.

Marlo? Prez said. You're saying *Marlo* freaked?

Listen, Carter said. You ever notice how long he's been at it? Marlo should have been done years ago. I mean, some guys only get a few runs, a dozen tops.

Right, Letterman said. Of course.

What? Prez said.

Shut up, Carter said.

Later, Carter's theory would make sense: if you live through a few runs and you keep running, you have to divide ever-increasing filaments of space to keep the rush, to make it worth anything. Sooner or later, you have to make the real decision, which isn't about beating the other guys. It's about whether or not you're really willing to die instead of losing against yourself. Although none of us had ever seen anyone get hit, we had heard the stories, one guy whose lower lip had been ripped clear off so he could never drink from a pop can again.

If you'd run, you'd know, Carter said to Prez.

I could see Prez turn deep red even in the dusk.

I never wanted to feel that way again. So I approached the edge of the road. I took my jacket off and held it loosely in my hand. I flexed my legs, waiting.

Whoooo! Carter said. O'Cleary's taking it on!

I remember the wind on my cheeks, the pump of my legs, how time slowed so I could feel each molecule of my body, think on how each atom had value. I thought of my dad, too, how they moved him to swing shift, the way he slept all day, his face pressed to the couch cushions so he woke with a red waffling on his cheek. And my mom, the endless click of her crochet hook. I wanted to save my own life. I wanted my life to be amazing. I dodged that minivan like a toreador.

In the daytime, though, at school and behind our building, I tried to figure out what happened to Marlo. I scanned the newspapers my father left scattered on the kitchen table each evening, looking for any news of a missing boy, but found nothing. Was Marlo too old to appear on a milk carton? I asked the guys: Couldn't you call him? Make sure he's alright? But nobody had a number. In fact, nobody seemed to know anything about him except the story Carter told: Marlo was the best player in Pontiac until Carter showed him up, or Letterman's story: Marlo had been teleported, was being tortured by aliens.

About a week into my time as a runner, my mom put her foot down, stood in front of the door as I was on my way out and said, Absolutely not. No way. She had spent the afternoon on the phone, and there was a boy missing. She couldn't stand it if she lost me.

I don't want you playing army games anyway, she said. There's better things for you.

Of course, faced with my mom's sensitivity and faith, I became even more certain I had to go. So I did what any guy would do: I said I was going to bed early and I climbed out the window.

The rest of us arrived to find Carter was already there. New order, he said.

What? said Letterman.

Old Marlo lost his edge. I never want to see that happen to any of us. So let's up the ante, Carter said, getting louder. Let's stay in the game. He held up a hanky and shook it, grinning. He rolled it and tied it over his eyes. Then, he drew from his pocket a small rectangular package we all recognized: the industrial-strength earplugs they gave our dads at work. Of course, our dads never wore them, so there were always pairs scattered around, the white cardboard grey with dust.

Christ on toast, Prez said. He's gonna walk out there like goddamned Helen Keller.

And he did. Three different cars dodged him, honked, but the moon was full that night and we could see that he was perfectly steady, didn't even flinch. Then he made his way back across.

A few other guys gave it a whirl, too, not wanting to be left behind. Letterman said he didn't want to wear the blindfold. He wanted to see the aliens before they took him to their leader. He wanted to see the universe opening itself if it was going to swallow him.

Pussy, Carter said.

So Letterman wore the hanky. It was soaked with sweat by the time he handed it to me.

I tied it over my eyes anyway, tipping my head to get a sliver of the ground. I put in the earplugs, too, already nasty from wax. I stepped out. I forced myself to go slowly. I watched for the yellow line. I felt my feet trip on the median's curb. Turning around, I had no idea that my angle was bad, no idea how close the call was when a Duster full of older kids hanging out the windows sped over the hill. But when it was through, the guys slapped me on the back, full of awe.

The thing was, though, nothing was ever enough. As the night wore on, we took greater and greater risks: spinning ten times first. Walking sideways. Backward. Counting to twenty, thirty, sixty as we crossed.

This isn't right, Prez said quietly while Carter was on his way back from a run in which he stopped at every tenth step for a count of ten.

What? I said, deeply out of touch with the obvious.

Prez turned toward the grassy field conspiratorially, so I turned with him.

He said, Marlo always told us the driver should see nothing more than a flash he can barely remember, like a spirit animal running in front of his car.

Yes, that was how it had felt the first time. But by then, a certain numbness had replaced the sheen. All day long I thought of running, but once I got there to do it, I didn't feel much of anything. I just ran.

A voice came from behind us: Why is it you're always running your mouth, but never running?

We turned. Carter held out the bandana in one hand, pointed at Prez with the other.

Prez swallowed, shook his head.

I wished, in that moment, that Prez could get beamed up.

Yes, said Carter. It's time.

No, Carter, I said. He's not ready.

It's alright, Prez said, slicking his hair back, shaking himself off as if he'd been rained on. I knew it was coming sooner or later. Why not tonight?

So Prez suited up, listened to Carter's list of rules. He stood at the side of the road for what felt like forever. He hovered his foot off the edge. From the other side of the hill, a high-pitched engine screamed. He put his foot down, started to walk. The car, a boxy little Cavalier, appeared, crested, and sped toward him. He turned to face it, his arms out, welcoming or blocking, I couldn't tell. He was there one minute, and then he was gone.

The part of me that had grown up over those weeks simply said, Game over. But this was Prez, the same Prez who walked his sister to the grade school every morning before he came to the Junior High. I had seen him teaching her to look both ways, to listen.

I ran into the road, but he was gone. I stared down at the place where he'd stood. There was nothing but a slick patch of oil I knelt down and touched.

When I came back in, my mom was sitting on my bed waiting for me, her face raw with crying. She tucked me in as if I were a small, small child, letting me press my forehead to her thigh, her hand on my back. And I was grateful, though I knew my dad, who was at work just then, would take care of me in the morning in a far less gentle way.

When I woke up, mom was in the kitchen winding the phone cord around herself, clutching at her neck. She hung up pale. A boy from the next building over had been hit by a car in the dead of night, she said. He'd been dragged all the way to Waterford. Worse, he'd lived through it. The driver had gotten away. And this so soon after that other boy disappeared.

They could have been you, she said, crying again. They could have been you.

My father came in then fresh from his shower and wearing his pajamas. He held his belt in one hand, a beer in the other. His eyes were tired. He pointed to my bedroom. I went willingly. Of course, a good thrashing isn't like being run over by a car. It's not like—whatever happened to Marlo. Lying facedown on my bed, as my dad's belt whistled through the air, I thought of the man in the Comet, his mustache. But I couldn't really remember his face anymore.

WOODS
[El Camino]

You stash things up in those woods they might not be there when you come back. All of us who hid things up there we couldn't keep at home lost something, followed our own paths back to find the hollow of an oak empty, rusty bucket overturned. Pack of GPC's missing the lucky. Bottle of Old Crow stolen from somebody's pops stolen again, drank down, black feathers on the label soaked by wet leaves, bird's eye rubbed off by eager fingers. Eager fingers down in those trailers and up in those woods, so what did it matter? Black dirt under the nails. Sour breath, anyway, and pleading.

My best almost-cousin Wanda lost it up there. To Jesse Walburn. Same place her sister lost it. Under the tarp stretched over what was left of the old El Camino, seat cushions long since eaten out by mice and the skinny deer crowded into those woods. A stunted grove of ash saplings pushed through its guts into the rusty hood, small grateful tendrils escaping to make mint green leaves in the spring, the kind that clap in the wind, shimmer.

Nobody knew how the car got there—how could someone drive it between the trees, whether down from the highway or up from the dirt road behind the trailers? Kids who played chase and hide-and-seek up there asked those kinds of questions. By the time we were fourteen, fifteen, we were out of questions and made-up answers, too. It was just part of those woods. Like the warped blue missile pits, empty red shotgun casings. A shelter that saved us from rain.

Before she left Carleton, up and left Michigan altogether, Wanda's sister warned us about Jesse trying to take our cherries, how good he was at talking a girl into it.

Wanda's family was nearly blood, had lived in the trailer next to ours since our grandparents' real houses got bought out by the government for the missile site. Our windows faced each other and even without phones Wanda and I could call each other in the night, which we did a lot when our brothers were away. Before they left they were just boys, still kid-skinny, but somehow able to keep our dads and uncles in check just by hanging around.

I wasn't at the party the night Jesse first started fixing to split our lives down the middle like the sweet maple up there'd been struck by lightning and opened. I stayed home on account of my brother being sick enough for the hospital, so I missed seeing exactly how it was Jesse got Wanda all the way to third base on his first try.

I remember watching as Mom put Denny in the car. I knew he couldn't see me because I was on the side where his eye turned up like a birth-clot. My palms were cold as I took my niece, Reba, into my arms.

The doctors never did anything, could never explain why Denny was fine one minute, collapsed and couldn't breathe the next. But when it got that bad we couldn't keep him at home, sit there and watch him die on the linoleum.

Bethany, my brother's girl, looked quick but deep into my eyes, nodded slightly, like she always did when she gave Reba over to me on a hospital run.

I nodded back and gathered Reba close.

Beth came up in those trailers, too, and we didn't need words. I was to keep Reba from my dad, who'd be home with us until his midnight shift at Fermi. I wouldn't go to sleep until he left, then I'd curl up in Beth and Denny's bed with Reba, watch the way her long black lashes fluttered on her cheeks while she dreamed. I'd pretend she was mine, despite the danger in that.

I was probably even glad for the occasional night off the party. You needed a good excuse not to go, something to tell whatever boy.

But because I wasn't there that September night it was Lori Walters who held Wanda's hair while she threw up, Lori who said, Jesse, you shit, she's too drunk to choose. Lori was three years older, was one of Jesse's first, so she could talk at him like that. But she couldn't stop it. Things happened fast up in those woods.

Lori came by the next morning and stood on our stoop. Right away I knew why, knew it had started. I didn't need to be told about Wanda on her knees in a thicket, warned about where it was headed and fast: El Camino. Shorthand for rupture, ruin.

All I'm saying's your girl might need an ear this morning, Lori said.

Soon as mom got home, I gave Reba up and snuck two Stroh's from the lean-to fridge, took Wanda to the woods. Damp Sunday morning, we tucked ourselves in the crotch the storm had given that big old maple. The break was already worn. You couldn't even see the scar anymore, the splinters having tossed themselves down and gotten swallowed by the earth, the bright yellow gone, just sap clinging to the back of our pants as we sucked off the beers, hair of the dog.

I don't even know how it happened, Wanda said. I remember more about puking him up with the whiskey after. She tried to laugh, tucked a piece of loose hair into her long brown braid.

I didn't know what to say. I wanted to make a plan, somehow invent a world where we could erase the night before. I wanted to comfort her, touch her hair, but I didn't know how.

Finally, Wanda said, Jesse's got the magic, though. Does he ever.

She said it to cover up, to make believe one night with Jesse meant she was ahead of me suddenly. Like she actually felt something for him, whatever it was we were supposed to feel for those boys who panted and scraped at us, so close to what happened at home we promised never to say out loud. I knew her well enough to know she was scared, both during and after. It was true we were coming apart, but that wasn't the reason, me not knowing how to want.

Jesse. Tall with a dry voice. The muscle in his cheek that twitched when he was thinking, when he bit his cigarette. My brother's best friend in junior high. They were still friends once in awhile, usually when Jesse wanted to smoke. That's probably half of what saved me. My brother Denny winking with his good eye, standing in the kitchen with his IV pole in one hand and a joint in the other saying, Don't even think about it, buddy.

No way, man. It's cool, Jesse said. His eyes wet and dark and watchful.

It was early summer. I stood at the kitchen window when he left. He stopped at the rose bushes and did like all the boys, laid a petal over his hollowed hand to pop it with the other palm, leave a slit up its middle. Other boys did it just because. He knew why he did it. He wasn't a boy, neither. He looked up at me through the glass grey with grease and smoke and smiled.

Once, when I was about ten and Denny was fourteen, walking in those woods on the ridge at the far edge near the highway, I spotted a grave marked by a tied-together cross, black shoelaces wrapped around and around. We knew the graves of animals, our pets, those killed on the road, and those hunted, were marked with heavy rocks out there, and we walked a wide swath around them. This was something else. Because we had no secrets from each other—just secrets we were all keeping together—and those woods were ours, we dug up the grave. We cleared the crumbling dirt from the plastic bag to find a rosary and a lock of hair, the newspaper photograph of a woman, *es que loca something* scrawled across the bottom just before the final word was melted by mud leaking in. It was wet up in those woods.

We got Gracie Alvarado to translate: *is it crazy*—what? To think he'd find the woman? This man who had her hair? Did she give it? Or did he steal it, the sicko?

That was the first time I saw and really understood, Gracie's belly out front like a basketball. She was fourteen. By the time her son was three everybody knew he was Jesse's—*if* we'd ever doubted it. Spitting image. Boy even had his swagger.

Jesse denied it, called Gracie a spic and a wetback. He was the same way about America Johnson, said, You think I'd screw a nigger?

He forgot that we were all there, we saw him push America up against a tree because my brother already had Bethany over in the El Camino. Not like Jesse claimed the white babies he made, either. I wanted something to change, especially for America's girl. But in a place like ours, I knew it wouldn't. By the time America's daughter was thirteen, there'd be another guy like Jesse, some kid who *was* Jesse's, too, to call his own sister more than bitch and slut after. I can't say if it was worse to be America than it was to be any of us because I don't know, but it couldn't have been better.

Gracie and America were thick as blood before all that, but after Jesse moved on from both of them, what was left of their friendship, that sisterhood like Wanda and I had? They stayed in their trailers changing diapers and twisting the phone cord while they waited for welfare to answer.

I didn't want to lose it in those woods. I wanted those woods for myself. When we found old things up there I felt like I lived in a real place. Plenty of arrowheads up there. Coins. And on one of the special walks we took before he left for Kuwait, Denny found a tiny black pair of girl's boots with what seemed a thousand eyelets for the laces. The kind someone might have worn in a covered wagon. Hanging in the crook of a tree for a hundred years, no doubt, and nobody happened to look sooner. You could never see everything about those woods, no matter how much time you spent looking.

Denny was getting worse, couldn't climb up there anymore. Nobody could figure out what was wrong with his brain or his nerves, fix his lungs rattling in the night. I needed those woods, took my time to them the way people take time to church. In the afternoon sunlight, the tarp over the car made a blue world, like breathing in a swimming pool. Then, I could almost forget the boys, Jesse, my brother's endless shakes. Plenty of times cutting school I curled there with a magazine and a candy bar, lost myself without drowning, woke cold but safe. As if I'd been asleep deeper than I slept at home.

I needed those woods so bad I almost lost it in the parking lot of the K-Mart—anywhere but trees—with Randy Vandler that summer, but we came up short, him wiping his mouth, saying, I can't do this. I think I still love Allie.

Allie was some girl from Keatington who'd never give it to Randy, I was pretty sure, but I felt relief spill into my chest, cool as the slurpees we bought and drank on the hood of his brother's Camaro, waiting for the stars to come out bright.

I pulled Wanda toward me on that old tree, told her again that we could go anywhere we wanted if we just didn't get knocked up.

What if you just stopped right now? I asked.

Guess I could, she said. But she didn't believe it. Jesse always finished what he started. He got to almost all of us. Letting him was just part of growing up in the trailers near those woods. And if he didn't want you, maybe there was something wrong with you.

After that day in the kitchen when I opened his beer, he watched me whenever we were all in those woods, his smile nothing of the coyotes that wailed on autumn nights, tore up the chicken coop we kept out back. But a coyote's just trying to make a living, to eat. A coyote couldn't hide so well, appear so toothless showing his teeth.

You really could, I said to Wanda, trying to make it true. Think about Beth.

But Wanda wasn't there, didn't feel Beth's hands clasping, hear her sudden cry. I was the one who sat with my brother's girl, warming her fingers as they emptied her body. She was *I-got-bigger-fish-to-fry-I-got-other-mouths-to-feed* brave until the chafe of paper sheets and speculum. Her face drained to white and the dark rings that came under her eyes in that moment never went away.

It was February, frozen, waiting for death to flood from the skin. Sleet blew through the parking lot where I tried to shield her from the posters. Half-formed and bloody babies seemed to dance on their pieces of wood above the hedges covered with slush.

No license, borrowed car, I drove her home to Reba who sat locked and wailing in her playpen, snot dripping to her wormish lip.

Bethany said to me, You know I'd keep it if we could. With the first one you think you can.

I never told Denny about the abortion. Bad enough Reba was born while he was gone. Bad enough he couldn't breathe anymore at night without a vent. The piercing wail of my brother's stopped chest invaded my dreams, left me running and running to find him up in those woods, in the desert of Kuwait, always a figure retreating, blocking out part of the sun.

I did tell Wanda about Beth, though, because we were pinky-swear friends. We told everything. It was because of Bethany we made the pact: we were never gonna, never with the boys around here and never up in those woods. Only if they married us first, liked us for other reasons.

But the way Wanda put on her makeup the night it happened told me that it would happen, anyway, pact or no. We stood in the bathroom before the party, her glopping CoverGirl onto her face, a shade darker than her skin. Extra green liner and shadow. When she turned to look at me I saw that her life was over. In Jesse's wake, there would be the others and soon she'd be the one twirling a phone cord around her finger, begging. Picking up boxes of powdered milk from the food pantry like our own moms had. I saw, too, that she had no choice.

If Jesse hadn't gotten to Wanda, everybody said later, she might have made it out.

I don't think so. There was something in Wanda, that's for certain. She was the only one in her family took regular classes at school, sat right next to me and endured the taunts of those Keatington girls.

Thing is, though, Wanda's brother didn't make it home.

Died doing a plow of Iraqi soldiers, Denny said. Burying hundreds of 'em alive was Shane's job over there. Never heard exactly, but bet he died on a run. Plenty guys did. Got swallowed up in their own trenches.

I wasn't too sorry. If brothers were no less awful than any other boy sometimes, Shane was worse than most. At least we were as strong as our brothers, had been fighting them long as we could remember, could bite and tear our way to freedom. But Wanda's dad kept hanging in the doorway of her room even after the war was over, six feet tall two-fifty. No one coming to stop it.

So she went up to those woods and I followed, found my hand in the hand of some boy whose name I can't remember now.

I watched as Jesse worked his magic around the fire, got everybody onto shots of nasty Hot Damn. It was November. Time of bittersweet vines, their berries the only red still singing. Even the patches of blood in the grass dried to brown. Those woods were no good for us in deer season until well after dusk when our orange-vested fathers poked around with shotguns, pouring salt on the ground, trying to put something out of its misery. Wanda's face shone as she disappeared into the El Camino with Jesse.

Those bent and gnarled young trees tangled in the guts of the car shuddered with its rocking, threw down their last clinging leaves.

The boy I was with put his hands up my shirt, fumbled under my bra. His cold fingers felt dead to me, like the innards of the deer dad and I'd butchered the day before.

Butchering was Denny's job before Kuwait, but after, it was mine. I held the leg of the doe firm for dad to saw through, his fingers covered in blood, slippery. He sunk them in at the top of her belly to see how fat she was. He cursed. The small pointed bone at the meeting of the ribs, busted by bullet, rested at my toes. I picked it up, felt its sticky warmth that had been so near the beating heart.

I felt the bone in the pocket of my jeans, pressing up against my hip under the boy's pressing. I shoved him away. Before he could reach out for me, cajole me to stay like they always did, I disappeared into those woods the way you could if they were part of you.

I wandered out to the missile pit where I found Lori Walters sitting on the edge smoking a cigarette, plucking the cotton out of a milkweed, letting it float on the air away. Quiet out there by those pits where for years the government prepared for Russia to bomb us. Scars and concrete in the ground. Now the atomic rot had gone back into the earth that swallowed everything, just like it had gone into my brother.

Lori was pretty quick and she probably knew why I was crying. She held me until I could breathe and offered me her smoke.

I know, I know, she said, soothing me. You try and try, but in the end, you can't decide the story of someone else's life.

I buried the piece of bone out there near the pit. I didn't want my mark to be as obvious as the cross we found out by the highway that time, me and Denny, or the forget-me-not letters buried by girls with plastic kiddie barrettes to mark them. Plenty of those up there, half of them probably for Jesse. Bright yellow bows or purple birds hard and unrelenting in the black dirt. I dug in, marked the grave of the doe I'd claimed as mine with a simple stone, near a tree I loved and knew well. Some curve in the stone, some pattern, a root breaking from the earth just so—I was sure I would never forget, that the map inside of me was stronger than any I'd ever seen on paper.

That was the last night I spent up in those woods until after I'd left for school, scholarship all the way down to Ohio State. Guidance counselor set it up for me when I told her I wanted out. I spent the last two years of high school studying and watching Reba while Bethany worked at the Super Wal-Mart that went in up on the highway and sitting quietly with Denny, who couldn't talk anymore, not even with his hands. Lou Gehrig's, we knew by then, just like all the other guys got over in the gulf.

I came home for Christmas that first year away at school, mostly to see him.

I saw Wanda, too. The edges of those woods were white, thick black branches poking up through the snowcover. Wanda stood with me there at dusk, snowflakes in her eyelashes. I couldn't bring myself to go in.

I'm pregnant, she said. Just two months.

The baby wasn't Jesse's, she was sure, but the guy's she ended up with after Jesse'd moved on to the next girl.

Get rid of it, I said. You'll ruin your life. Words like armor-piercing bullets covered with uranium Denny said came *so hot and fast sand turns to glass when they hit.*

My love for Wanda turned her into something else. And being away turned me into someone else. I forgot how babies brought hope to a place like ours, right or wrong. I forgot how only birth and death could gather us all together. I forgot the way everything dangerous eventually sealed over—the missile pits filled up with so much sand you couldn't dig your way in, the old carpet we dragged up to those woods to make a fort covered with moss, and friendships mended by the pressure of space and just plain tiredness. Growing up in those trailers near those woods leaves you tired, even after you take off from there for good, when you only come back for funerals.

Beth finally got brave enough to pull the plug the spring I turned twenty-three. In front of the altar of St. Joe's, under the plaster Christ hanging on his cross, they laid my brother out in his full dress uniform, collar pulled up to cover his neck. I could remember the first time he wore it, the way his muscles filled the sleeves when he reached down to hug me. But by the time he died, the jacket was baggy, had to be pinned behind him.

Jesse Walburn stood near my brother's body with a terrible look on his face, deep lines cutting his forehead, a single streak of grey at his temple. He wasn't even thirty. Still lean, long, loping as he walked down the aisle toward the door, his throat bobbing like he'd choke.

Lori Walters left her kids and husband in back, came and sat right behind me when the priest started talking bullshit. She put her hand on my shoulder and kept it there until my muscles eased up.

Wanda was in back with her kids, too. She waited on the front step in the bright spring sun and hugged me. She felt smaller in my arms than I remembered, more solid. We ate egg salad and pork chops side by side in the rented hall afterwards, just like we did after we looked at her brother's casket—except, that one was empty, no hands crossed over the heart.

At the end of the night, everybody went home except the ones who knew Denny up in those woods. Lori, always on her game, matriarch of our ragtaggle tribe, put on an old Bruce Springsteen cassette and cranked it up and everybody started to dance.

This is what Denny would have wanted, Lori said.

I watched as Jesse danced with girls who would have killed him five years back, before they were resigned to their fates, found other daddies for their babies or dropped them off at the church daycare.

He came over to Wanda, asked her to dance.

Sure, she said, grinning and handing me her plate.

Right, I thought, they might not go up into those woods anymore, but they live together in those trailers. They see each other at the Super Wal-Mart and they dig each other's cars out of the snow. They know each other in a way no one will ever know me again.

Wanda laughed and smacked Jesse on the arm over something. They walked over to me together. He took my hand, pulled me in. I let him because I thought I'd fall down if he didn't hold me up. In my mind, I could see him and Denny leaning against the kitchen counter, sipping off their beers, laughing. My brother's head tipped back, neck long and smooth, before the metal clasp and tube.

Jesse took me to the dance floor. He bent down to hold me, his arms like a brief vice around my arms and shoulders. Wiry, nothing like Denny's.

The night was over. The song was over. Denny was dead. It was time to let go and we both knew it. But I did not let go of Jesse. He looked down at me, looked right into my eyes.

So? he asked.

I was tired. I let him lead me to the door where America Johnson and Gracie Alvarado stood watching their kids dance together. Brother and sister.

Where you off to? Gracie said to us.

America just shook her head. Hopeless, her eyes seemed to say.

Wanda stared at me long and hard from across the room. I kept her eyes a few seconds, saw them flash a warning in the old language. I went anyway.

In the parking lot, a light rain fell. I got into Jesse's truck and let him drive me over to those woods. I knew it was where he would go. And how I had craved it all that long time away. We parked his car on the trailer side, behind the pile of unused culverts that had been there so long no one remembered what they were meant to drain. In the full moon they were gaping mouths rising from the ground.

Jesse and I went up, in. Soon as I felt the magic there, the familiar air, I stripped off my coat. My skin prickled with relief, like I was a puzzle piece that finally found its way to the empty spot, my edges soothed by being held in somewhere for a time. Spring in those woods was wild, the new green something thick as blood poured all over the night, all over Jesse Walburn as he stood next to that El Camino.

This is what it would have been like, I told myself.

But it wasn't. I wasn't fourteen, fifteen. I was a woman and I knew how to turn my body toward him, relax the small of my back to let him enter. Inside of me he was dull, thudding, an old score settled passionless for everybody, our clothes tangled around our ankles, the ridges of metal pushed into my back. I was cold. There was no magic when he came, no agony of something lost, just Jesse, who was nothing more than a guy from my hometown who didn't know how to do it any better than this, finishing the woods of my girlhood, those woods I'd already lost buried inside my chest so it felt like I would cry, choke up wet branches, leaves, a pair of girl's boots.

We lay for a few minutes, wordless. Then I pulled my jeans back up. I slipped out of the El Camino and began to walk away.

Hey, wait up, he said.

See you around, I said. I needed to look for what I'd buried, touch myself at fifteen.

In the dark I moved from tree to tree, seemingly guided by the moon itself. Jesse held out his lighter so I could examine the bark of a particular tree. I touched stone after stone. But I didn't remember exactly. Nothing was really familiar. It only seemed I knew those woods. I felt something haunting my chest, something breaking.

You need a hand? Jesse said, following me as I thrashed up toward the highway. He was polite, worried, ruined for me.

All along I had dreamt of other places, didn't want to stay in those trailers, and in that moment, groping for what I already knew was lost, just another dead thing under a rock, I realized that getting out really was an accident. Luck, if such a thing exists. It could have gone either way. Of course, I was already safe, so it was easy to admit.

In the morning, Wanda came over with the kids, brought me a mug of coffee. She didn't say a word about it. She was the wise one that morning and I was the stupid girl. We sat on the porch, watching the kids run through the puddles that had formed in the grass, water coming down from those trees in the night. She stroked my hair, the way we had always grieved together, piled into the El Camino with her sister, old magazines and licorice sticks, a hand tangled or braiding, saying, You can endure. You can. You will make it through.

How's life? I asked. It was all I could think to say.

It's decent, she said. She tapped two cigarettes out of her pack and offered me one, cupping her hand around mine to light it.

Our eyes talked in the old way, bleeding and accepting apologies in less time than it took to blow clouds of smoke in the air, bite down and clap as Wanda's oldest son, the one I tried to erase, held out his arms to fly.

BREAKNECK ROAD

[*Reliant*]

Walking home from Country Lake Liquor I see a red something there between the snowbank and the line of grey slush left by the plow: Coca-cola box, the long tail on the C poking through the loop on the L. I almost kick it the way you do a thing on the roadside, make it fly and hit the ice on the edges of the swamp. But something stops me. Maybe hope gets to me. Even in this weather, a little something sweet to put with the 151. So I go and lift the flap. Even looking at it I don't buy what's inside that box: human baby, tiny, almost blue, curled up and no bigger than a skinned muskrat. Dead baby. But no, it's breathing. The nostrils flare and its hand opens just a little bit and slow like one of those stop-action flowers on PBS.

What can a person do with a baby in a box when he's no friend to the law? Especially once the thing opens its black-hole eyes and looks right at him like it's accusing him?

I don't even think about Cherry and what she'll say. I drop my bag and take up the box. The cardboard is wet and collapses where I touch it. I don't know what women do with babies, but it's colder than fuck out and the thing doesn't have a little sweater or anything. I tear one side of the box off quick. And like those climber guys who stripped naked in their tent to save their frozen friend in the Arctic and didn't even care that the whole world saw it on the television, I lift my flannel and press the whole soggy deal to my skin.

Right away the thing starts to wriggle. Then, it expands and yowls fit to beat a bag of mad cats because I don't have tits and that's what it wants most likely.

Shhhh, I say, like it knows how to behave.

I look around to make sure nobody's watching. I've never seen a soul but the plow out on Breakneck this time of year and I can tell that prick Randy's already been by. But sometimes even when you aren't doing anything wrong, you don't want to be seen. The thing's having a hissy fit loud enough now to reach the horizon, all those houses cozied up on real streets, houses for folks who work at Great Lakes Coal, same ones I got busted for three winters back.

My bag's melted, so I grab my rum and the hotdogs Cherry's mom wanted and pick up my pace. I walk that baby right to the trailer, get us in the lean-to, and start stripping off wet layers. And that's what I'm doing when Cherry finds me, standing there in my fruit-of-the-looms peeling red cardboard off this screaming cheesy baby. It's a boy, his nutsack bright pink and enormous, his penis uncut. Where his belly-button should be is a purple snake tied with a yellow yarn. Other than that, he's all set, ten fingers and toes, no frostbite, sticky black hair, and a voice like a damned opera singer. Between the kid and the TV blaring in the back room where Cherry's mom's watching, Cherry can't hear me trying to tell her what happened. Of course she's talking over everything I say, anyway, so it all comes out in a jumble.

Are you insane, Joe? You can't just pick up a baby like a stray dog.

I come into the kitchen, elbowing my way past her. The kid's slippery and I'm trying to figure out how to hold him without breaking him or flopping him around too much. His skin's a hell of a lot colder than a living baby's skin ought to be.

I mean, somebody's got to do it, Joe, but it can't be you, Cherry says. It sure can't be you.

Cherry blows the smoke from her cigarette through her nostrils like a dragon and starts to pace on the other side of the counter. She's done near worn a hole in the carpet over the last few years between me and her mom.

It ain't legal. It ain't clean, she says.

I know it ain't clean, Cherry, I tell her. I'm about to give it a bath if you'll just give me a hand.

I hold the kid out toward her. His arms and legs fly out like he's skydiving and his cries are fast and raspy. Desperate.

Oh, no, Cherry says. She shakes her head and holds up both her hands palms out, her cigarette ash falling on the floor. I'm not having anything to do with it.

I stop and look at her for a long minute the way I do when I want her to know just how unreasonable she's being, but she's making a point not to look at me or the baby. I shrug. I wad the boy up and tuck him in the crook of my arm like a bundle of firewood. He arches his back and lets out a fresh series of howls. I struggle to plug the sink with my free hand. I turn on the tap. Water's ice cold. Out in the swamp we don't get much hot.

It's kidnapping, that's what, Cherry says. She lights a new cigarette off the one she's smoked down.

Jesus, Cherry, I say. I didn't sneak into its crib and steal it, for Chrissakes.

Joe!

Cherry raises her cigarette hand like she'll smack me. Apparently, there's no situation that warrants taking the Lord's name in vain.

I rummage around in the cabinet for a pot, take a deep breath, and try again: Somebody left it, I say over the ruckus. He was just sitting there alongside—

You go out looking for trouble you're bound to find it.

Yeah, Cherry, I say, practically yelling now, jamming the pot under the faucet. Uh-huh. That's right. I woke up this morning and says to myself, what could make my shit life even better?

I juggle the pot against my hip the way I've seen Cherry do. I slam it on the stove, sloshing water all over. I crank up the burner, careful not to roast the kid's toes. Then I turn to Cherry like I'm in a soap opera and slap myself on the forehead.

Oh! Of course! A baby. Why didn't I think of it sooner? And so I head out hoping to find one. And lo and behold, there just happens to be a baby freezing its ass off right in my path. Lucky, lucky me!

But the truth is, I do feel a little bit lucky. It's not like this shit happens to just anybody. I look down at the little guy. Cherry's pretty faithful to the pill and we're always broke, so we might not have any of our own. I've never seen a lot of babies up close. Outside of the gunk that's stuck all over him and the noise he's making, he's kind of cool. Hard to believe you could start off like this and end up nearly forty, hairy, drooping, nothing to show for it but a parole officer and a trailer owned by your girlfriend's mother.

I wipe off my pinky finger on the kitchen towel and offer it up to the kid the way I once saw this guy do with his baby way back in high school. When the boy takes my finger, his sound is shut off like a stereo when the circuit's blown. The kid settles in that way, crosses his arms and legs over his body. The roof of his mouth is ridged and he sucks mightily, his eyes wide and hopeful.

I feel you, buddy, I say. I wish I had three arms so I could get to that 151 and have a pull myself.

You could get busted, Cherry says, turning off the tap. You could go back to jail. Or even prison if somebody thinks you done something wrong to it. She glances at my finger suspiciously, preparing her testimony, no doubt. Then she looks away. I can tell she didn't really see the boy, didn't notice how . . . human he is.

Now that the kid's quiet I can hear the announcer on The Price is Right from the other room shouting: Let's see what's behind door number three, Johnny!

A brand new baby, I say, stepping into Cherry's path. Come on, Cherry, I say. Have a heart.

You picked it up, Joe, Cherry says. You're the one that touched it.

What was I supposed to do?

The boy's caught on that my finger doesn't make milk and he cranks up his wailing again. This time it's a jagged series of cries precipitated by enormous inhales.

What's that racket? Cherry's mom rasps from the back room. The station must be on a commercial break because she's muted it and I hear the creak as she hauls herself up onto her walker.

For the first time, Cherry looks at me. I can see that she's working it out with me, trying to get our story straight. We struggle together like that. The edges of her eyes are like the woods that surround the swamp. You could get lost there if you don't know where you're going. But I can see I'm on a path.

That first summer out of jail Cherry had me trap a mess of raccoons that were raising hell under the trailer nights. She hated them even as she ate the damned stew. Then, when only the one baby raccoon was left, she up and took him in. Just for the night, she said. Thing lived with us for a month or two—until it tried to wash a couple of joints in the toilet bowl. It escaped when I gave chase. The look on that animal's face when it saw there was a whole world outside of the pre-fab one! It gave a little fuck-you-very-much sneer and waddled off into the swamp, no doubt stoned as Steve Miller from the few soggy bites of pot it ate before I caught it. Cherry was heartbroken.

I hold the flailing baby out like an offering, my hands cupped under his butt and shoulders. He claws wildly at his own face and it hits me just how helpless he is, how close the call was. He really would have died out there. Maybe the coyotes would have come after dark. I feel a sick panicky tingle in my bladder. There would have been no trace. A whole life could happen, and never happen, at the same time.

I mean, what would Jesus do, Cherry? For real?

She barks a quick laugh. But then she glances at the crucifix on the wall and clutches at her necklace. The boy's chest rises and falls over his squalling. It's enough to wear on a saint. Even one like Cherry, who sighs and rolls her eyes, which is always how she starts her giving in. Right from our first time in the back seat of the old Plymouth Reliant I inherited from my dad it was like this. She shakes her head. Then she bites her cigarette and takes the baby into her arms.

Out of the corner of her mouth she says, Fine, then. But you know, you ain't Jesus, Joe. You're gonna have to turn it in to the cops eventually, and that means talking to the cops and that means—

Look, Cherry, I say. Least you could do is find him a towel or a blanket or something. And you want to put out that cigarette?

Who died, she says, and made you the American Cancer Foundation? But she tosses her smoke into the ashtray.

She and the kid disappear together into the hallway, but I can pinpoint exactly where they are by listening. The bathroom door closes and the cabinet opens, muffling the kid's noise. I hear Cherry trying to soothe him: What's the matter? What's the matter, baby?

Stupid question. He's cold and hungry. So am I, come to think of it.

I go out on the porch to take a leak and retrieve the bottle of 151 I left tucked in the snowbank. I unscrew the cap and drink deep and long. The slight sleet pelts my bare skin. I feel incredibly alive. The snow, the dark break in all the white where the swamp's melted through, it all seems more important now, somehow.

I'm hiding the bottle in the siding next to the fuse box when Pauline comes clanking in, dragging her oxygen tank with her. She cocks her head toward the muffled sounds of Cherry trying to sing the theme song from *Gilligan's Island*. Pauline's hair, which is done up in front with lots of hairspray, is flat and matted in the back, the cord from her oxygen pressed around it. Her lipstick is bright red and uneven under the clear plastic mask. I think she's going to ask me what in hell's going on, but she just holds her hand out. I pass her the bottle. She pulls the mask off her face and takes a swig.

Pauline covers her face again, heaving. That a baby crying? she asks between drags of oxygen.

I don't answer. It's best if people handle their own mothers. I tuck the bottle away and secure the latch on the fuse box. I get a dry pair of long johns from the closet and haul them on. I go over and look at the water, but it's not boiling yet. Come on, I pray at it.

Cherry comes into the kitchen. She's got the boy wrapped in my robe. She's looking down into the boy's face. There's something in the flush of her cheeks I've seen but can't place just now.

That's what I thought, Pauline says. She shuffles over to the boy and draws back the folds of terry cloth. No more'n a few hours old, she says. Where'd he come from?

Somebody left him, Cherry says, looking up with tears in her eyes. Can you imagine?

It's love. I'll never know what happened to Cherry in that five minutes she was alone with the kid, but maybe it was like what I felt when I was hoofing it home. The universe chose me. Us.

Truth be told, Cherry's always been a little funny in this way.

Josie Sigler

Example? She knew me since we were kids—I grew up on the other side of Breakneck. Anyway, she must've refused me twenty times in all those years. Then, she shows up at my door one night wearing a triple-fat winter coat over her nightgown. Says her momma's sick and will I drive them to Monroe Mercy because it's snowing and she's too scared. Of course I do. After I drop them off, I leave east and hit all the houses I can find empty down by the riverfront just in case it's any kind of date we're on and I need the cash. I'm taking a nap in the Reliant when she opens the door. She presses her nightgown against me. And two months later I go to jail and even though it goes far above and beyond the call of grateful, she sticks with me through the whole thing.

Sure, says Pauline. People are shits.

Mom!

It's true, she says. She laughs the laugh of the lungless and holds out her finger to shake the little guy's hand.

When the first folds of steam rise from the pot I pour some hot water into the cold water in the sink until it's just right, and Cherry hands me the baby and a fresh washcloth.

Watch so his belly-button don't get wet, now, Pauline says as I slide him into the sink. And support his neck.

The boy's suddenly more turtle than human, his arms and legs coming out one by one as Cherry moves the washcloth over them. He's quiet now but for some small hoarse hiccupping noises. He seems to like the water. When Cherry's gotten all the mess off him, I pull him out and swaddle him in a couple of dishtowels.

Cherry puts the steaming pot back on the stove, finds the hotdogs, opens the package, and drops them in.

He needs something, too, I say.

Milk? Cherry says.

We ain't got none, I say, feeling bad for buying the 151 when I could've bought milk.

Momma always said sugar water'd keep a little one a few hours, Pauline says.

How do I get it in him? I ask.

Straw? Cherry says.

Cherry mixes the boy a drink and I sneak another myself. I can't find a straw, so Pauline volunteers a piece of her tubing. I unplug her briefly, cut a bit with Cherry's nail scissors, and go to work feeding the boy. I draw up a few drops of sugar water at a time. I put the tube in his mouth. He sucks again and again and cries between rounds. It takes forever. And the whole while I'm feeling bad that the kid's first meal is so shoddy. Deep inside I hear myself promising him that it won't happen again.

The boy yawns, rests his head on my collarbone, stares at me again with his huge eyes. I watch the pulse in the small sunken diamond on the top of his head. I feel a bit sleepy myself. But the sun is going down. I hear the late plow coming up Breakneck a second time. The boy's pee has sunk through the towels and into my leg hairs real good. I realize no matter what the weather's like and how broken the Reliant is I've got to go out and get the things the boy needs.

With what, Cherry says, your good looks?

Money's a rough point between us, especially since Cherry lost her job about six months back and the unemployment's about to run out. I was never able to get in down at the plant or even any of the auto plants up in Detroit. No diploma. Born too late. Last job I had was over a year ago now, painting houses with my cousin. Even he had to let me go. People complained. Seriously, once you figured out I was the one broke into all those people's houses, would you want me to stack all your stuff in the middle of the room under a tarp?

On top of this, I've missed my last two phone calls with my parole officer. I haven't gone to the AA meetings, either. No good reason besides I got traps to check, a furnace that breaks twice a week, and I don't like people up my ass. I know the cops won't come down to the swamp unless I really fuck up. So I've been pretty committed not to go past Country Lake Liquor if I can help it. But this is going to require a trip up to the Wal-Mart out on the highway because I don't think the liquor store has diapers and even if they do, how will I explain why I need them?

I shift the baby into Cherry's arms and stand up. I walk out to the lean-to and start to get bundled to head back out.

Cherry follows me, the boy passed out on her tits.

Joe, she says.

I ignore her, haul on my boots and rummage around for my hat. I'll miss the plow if I don't hurry.

Joe! she almost yells.

You're gonna wake him, I say. I fumble around on the top shelf for the gloves with leather fingertips and my kit.

Cherry says, Maybe we shouldn't go buying him things. Maybe we should leave him at the church or the police station or something. Maybe we should do it tonight so we don't get too attached to him.

She says all of this looking down into his face like she's the mother of God.

Sure, maybe, I say. Then I wait.

Or maybe we could keep him just one night, she says.

Leaving him in the cold like that, I say. That would make us no better than his parents, right?

She won't say so. She just clutches him a little tighter.

And of course I don't mention that I'll have to hit a house or two to afford the shit because she'll never have to know. I'll tell you this: almost nobody's as good at what they do as I am. I can slip into any house so seamless that it doesn't matter how many I have to hit in one week. I don't get a thrill out of it like some of the guys I met in jail. It's just a job. I never take anything big, anything more than I need, anything someone would notice missing until much later. There's a whole class of people, in fact, who are always wondering: where did that last twenty go? And they think they lost it. I'm here to tell you: they didn't. Somebody smoked their last Pall Mall. Somebody made a sandwich in their kitchen while they were in the john. I steal like their own kids, like the wife who needs an extra ten for a dozen eggs and a loaf of bread.

The only time I slipped up was when they put Pauline on that Coumadin before her Medicaid came through. That was right after Cherry and I hooked up and I wanted to impress her. So for two weeks straight I took any dime I could get my hands on. Love-stupid, I guess. I swore it was my last gig. I was going to look for a real job before Cherry got suspicious about how I made my money. Of course, she knew. She always knows.

I walk out to the road just in time. Randy nods at me through the icy window of his truck and swings it toward me. I hop over the plow as it slides past, open the door and climb in. The truck smells of booze and the cheap cigarillo he's got clutched in his teeth.

How's it goin', man?

Good by me, I say. The baby's not really a story I can tell, though Randy and I go way back to grade school. He's always been kind of an asshole, but gave Cherry a real hand when I was in the clink, coming over to chop wood and all. Randy's got a record, too. Statutory, about ten years back. He took over running the plow for the county when his dad died. Cancer in the balls. Must have been a rough storm, too, because my old buddy looks like hell. His stubble is going grey a lot faster than mine and his eyes are bloodshot like he's been drinking heavy. I been there myself, so I don't think anything of it. We used to drink together, sometimes, back when I drank with other people.

Where you headed? Up to Country Lake?

Naw, man. I need to get out to the highway.

Sure thing, he says. Headed out there after I hit Miller one last time. Roads are a shitty mess. Been everywhere today twice.

Gotta grab a few groceries at Wal-Mart, I say. A few things for Cherry, I add.

Gonna hit the parking lot up there later, he says, if you need a ride back.

Be great, I say. Might have my hands full.

Sure thing, he says. He crushes his cigarillo in the ashtray and reaches over my knees to get into the glove compartment. He brings out a baggie of weed and papers and dangles it in front of my face with one hand while he maneuvers the truck at the intersection to shove a new pile of snow against the bank. His fingernails are thick-crusted with power-steering fluid or rust. Seems the dude's truck is shitting the bed on top of I heard his girl walked out on him, too, a few months back.

Naw, man. It's cool, I say, as he lifts the plow and puts the truck in reverse.

Roll me one?

I take the baggie and get down to business. My mouth waters at the smell of it, but tonight's not the night to get fucked up. If it's my one night to do right by the kid, I'd like to do it. By the time Randy gets us to the highway, I've rolled him an acceptable joint. He lights it right there at the intersection, inhaling deeply. He hands it to me, but I hold my hand up.

You sure, man?

Yep. Cherry'll blow a gasket.

Women, he says, shaking his head. Women, women, women!

He's in fine form. Like I said, I've been there, so I don't pay attention to how off he is. He slides into the Wal-Mart parking lot.

I jump out.

Meet you back here in an hour or so? he says. He blinks, trying to focus on my face.

Thanks, buddy, I say. An hour oughtta do it.

I watch as he skids out of the parking lot. I guess he's gotten a little loose around the bolts. I think prison must do that to a guy and I was lucky to get jail time instead. I was lucky my dad just up and disappeared instead of dying slowly right before my eyes.

You can't steal directly from Wal-Mart too often these days or they catch you on their cameras. So once Randy's out of sight, I double back, jog across the highway to the fancy suburb that's grown up around the Wal-Mart. I walk along the edge of the forest like I'm headed home. I slip into the trees. It's the first secret of both hunting and stealing, my dad taught me. Think like a tree. Move so slowly no one knows you're moving. Be part of the landscape.

This time of day in winter is amazing because it's already pitch black out and nobody's home from work yet. This neighborhood's always been a great deal for a thief, too, because it's a cross between what we've got in the swamp, places to hide, and what they've got in town: neighbors. You can stand in the trees for hours and wait to make your move. You can hit more than one house.

The backdoor of my first house faces the woods and has your standard pickable locks. All the houses here work pretty much the same and the people are predictable, too: in about sixty seconds, I'm robbing yet another guy who keeps a safe-deposit box in the closet and the key in his bedside drawer. Sure enough, there's an emergency fund. Plenty for me to take forty and not have the family starve if suddenly they run out of canned green beans and peaches in syrup. I open the guy's closet to see if he has more than one pair of hunting socks. He does. Score. I sit on the edge of the bed and double up so my feet are warm and snug. I wipe the floor near the door with the towel I carry in my kit. I grab an apple from the fruit bowl. Then I get the hell out of dodge.

Back in the woods, I check my watch. Six minutes. Not bad for an old guy. I'm thinking forty bucks will do it when I pass a house with the living room lit up so I can't help but see a woman handing a baby not much bigger than our boy to a man wearing a button-down shirt and a tie, just home from work, no doubt.

I stand there eating my apple, watching. The man makes a big excited face like the baby is the most surprising thing he's ever seen. Faker. The mother leans over and kisses the baby's feet. Then they settle into the couch, the three of them, and they look like one body. I get closer. The guy holds out the remote, turns on the TV to reveal a newscaster standing in front of a giant map of Michigan, shoving another big storm forward with his hands. Bastard.

I walk down to the window on the end of the house, the one I know looks in on the smallest room. I want to see what kind of stuff these people have for their baby. Light from the hallway falls on the crib that looks more like a little prison with a mobile dangling over it. There's a high table stuffed with clothes. I put my fingers on the window and push up slightly. It's locked. These people always think that will stop a guy. Then they leave keys under fake rocks near their back doors. I slide along the edges of the house, gently turning each stone. I find the key under the ceramic sunflower near the back door.

I let myself into the far door, which leads me down into the basement. This one's unfinished, the same kind of dank grey basement I'd retreat to for hours in my twenties waiting for someone to go to sleep or leave again. I take my towel and work at getting my boots dry. Listening to make sure the TV is still on, I creep up the stairs. Stupid as a spring chicken but slick as butter, I go to the kid's room. I check for a place to hide should somebody come in. No place, so I lock the door from inside. People always think they've accidentally done this themselves, and it gives you an extra minute to get out the window.

Josie Sigler

I pull the little flashlight out of my kit and look at the stuff that's on the table. Big pink bottle of lotion. Plastic container of wipes. Aloe-scented. On the second shelf, there's a whole stack of tiny shirts, about twenty. I unfold one to see that they have snap-on underwears attached. I pull two out of the stack. Two pairs of socks. Then I hit paydirt—I find a tiny set of red long johns in the very back near the bottom. It's risky, for sure. My dad always said: Never take anything that's one of a kind. But a kid living out near the swamp is always gonna need thermals more than a kid who lives in the land of central heating. On the side shelf there's a stack of small blankets with different animals on them. I pull one from the stack, giraffes. I toss the rest of my loot in it, roll it up, tuck it down the front of my pants, cover my crotch with my flannel, and get the hell out of dodge.

Ten minutes later, I'm wandering the endless rows of diapers in the Wal-Mart feeling like I've got the biggest set of balls in Monroe. I get the diapers that say *newborn*, two blue plastic bottles, *improved natural suction*, and ten cans of formula, *gentle*. I get Cherry a carton of smokes and pick up Pauline's prescriptions. I roll my cart up to a checkout manned by some girl too young to know me and ask questions. By the time Randy's sliding into the handicap space, I'm standing out front waiting with my bag like I'm his wife or something.

Thanks, man, I say, climbing into the cab.

You betcha, he says. He pulls onto the highway, driving over the snow and ice like it isn't even there.

Everything goes along fine until the plow skids out on a patch of ice near Breakneck and my bag tips to the side and one of my cans of formula rolls out onto the seat.

Randy looks down at it. What in hell's that? he asks.

Can of milk, I say, catching it in my left hand and stuffing it back in the bag.

Yeah, but ain't that baby milk? he says.

I pretend to examine it. Shit, I say. I must have grabbed the wrong thing by accident.

Randy shakes his head, shuddering. That's so weird, he says.

Yeah, I say.

He looks at me funny when he drops me on Breakneck, like he

wants to ask me something more about it, but he doesn't. I reach out and shake his hand.

See ya, buddy, I say.

In the house, it's all chaos again. Cherry's pacing by the door. She nearly throws the kid at me when I walk in.

He's starving, she says. You were gone forever.

She and Pauline make the boy a bottle, boiling nipples and warming formula. I get him all dressed up in a diaper, a pair of socks, and one of those T-shirts. The crotch comes nearly to his toes. I fumble with the snaps. Then I pull on his long johns. The arms and legs hang past his feet and fingers. But at long last, the four of us sit on the couch together. I touch the nipple of the bottle to the kid's lips and he hooks right on.

Pauline pulls her mask away from her face. You ask me, she says, I think it's a message from the universe or something. A gift.

Then she gets all choked up. Pauline's lived one hell of a life of drinking and whoring, paid for that trailer with blood and sweat and turned out four decent kids, and I've never seen her get weepy about anything. Her breathing and the boy's suckling make a nice rhythm. Cherry puts her arm around my neck. Everything is so perfect I never want it to end. I keep picturing stripping him back down, handing him over to the cops, trying to make up answers to their questions about something they can't understand.

That night, the boy sleeps between us for the first time. We take turns watching him, feeding him. I thump his little back and pace the room with him. Snow and wind rock the trailer, but it's as if we're safe in the hull of a great ship.

When the sun comes up orange in the room Cherry's sitting by the window, staring out at the snow.

He'll end up going to fosters, she says.

After my dad left and my mom died I went to the system. I remember how one of those fosters liked to whip us kids out by the leaf-burning barrel in the fall. How I snuck off. How I could sneak off because my dad taught me the skills to fend for myself in any economy.

Look, I say. If its own parents did this to it, how do we know some foster family's gonna be any better? The only chance this kid has is us. We're his chance.

They'll never choose us, Joe, she says. She raises her arm and points to the wall, to me, to herself as if our very existence is proof enough. Never, she says.

Yeah, Cherry, but how will anyone ever know the baby's not ours to begin with? You been home now for months. How could anyone say you weren't knocked up the whole time?

I press Cherry to me. She doesn't say anything for a long while. Finally she makes some small noise deep inside that I hear. And I know we aren't going to take the boy to town. We aren't going to sell him out. And in that moment, I love Cherry Jenkins more than I ever have in all the years since I was ten.

For the next few weeks, we hardly do a thing that isn't about the boy. We settle into a real routine with him. Cherry watches him in the early mornings when I go to the swamp to check my muskrat traps. He sleeps on my chest all afternoon. Cherry keeps him in the evenings if I have to go out. I get up with him in the night. I'm hardly drinking at all. Before we know it Pauline's referring to herself, in the third person, as Grandma. As in: Grandma is gonna give the baby boy a big old kiss oh yes she is! We've tested calling the boy Joey. It hasn't quite caught on, maybe because we're still scared.

The next ice storm is a real doozy and the generator ices over. The plow thrashes outside and I wish for the second or third time that folks would find another way out to the highway, leave Breakneck alone. Finally, on his third pass, Randy parks the plow down at the end of our driveway and starts walking up.

What're we gonna do? Cherry says.

We're still trying to figure out how to introduce the boy in town, get our story straight. In winter, if you live out in the swamp, no one really bothers after you. You never even see your neighbors. But once it gets to be March, you don't emerge, people might start thinking you've been done in by the gas heater.

Maybe we just tell him, Cherry says.

I look at Pauline, who's got the same gut I do. She hooks her thumb toward the back of the trailer. It's been a rough day for her breathing because she can't do a nebulizer without electricity.

Go to the bedroom, I say to Cherry. I toss her a bottle I've been warming in my armpit. It's not quite warm enough, but it'll have to do. Keep him quiet, I say. Your mom and I can handle this.

I nod at Pauline, who nods back.

I know Randy's thinking we'll ask him in and give him a drink and I can't think of a way to say no. Everybody out by the swamp gives the plow guy a drink. It's tradition. So while Cherry scurries off, I open the door and Randy stomps in, tracking snow all over the carpet.

How's it goin', buddy? Ain't seen you in a coon's age!

Good enough, I say, slapping him on the back.

It's getting late and we've only got a few candles lit so I'm hoping he doesn't notice all the baby stuff scattered around.

It's a shitty mess out there, he says, slapping me back. When he raises his arm I can smell that he hasn't showered. His beard has grown and there's food in it. Being a bachelor, I think, does not suit this guy. He reeks of booze, lurches forward when I bring out cups.

Want a little sniff of something? I ask.

Sure thing, he says.

I start working at the fuse box, rummaging around to find the hollow. But I'm nervous, and I knock the bottle down inside the paneling. It smashes onto the concrete foundation.

A muffled wail goes up in the bedroom.

Randy looks in the direction of the noise. That a baby? he asks, his eyes widening.

I look at Pauline again, but her eyes are turned toward the ceiling as if to say: What can you do? You have to tell him now.

Sure is, buddy, I say.

He's a drunk. Maybe he won't remember or think much of it.

A baby, he says. Whose?

Well, ours, of course, I say. Then I yell to Cherry: Bring Joe Jr., out for a minute, hon, so Randy can see.

Cherry comes creeping from the hallway, terrified. I tip my head to the side, tighten my lips. Calm down, I mouth.

Since when you got a baby? Randy snorts. You was in my plow a month ago with baby milk falling out your bag saying you didn't have no baby.

So much for the theory that drunks don't remember things.

I'm fumbling around behind the fusebox again, hoping beyond hope that Pauline hasn't gotten the rest of my stash. But she's shaking her head no, pointing to the space behind the fridge. I go over, start digging there.

Sure we do, Randy, Cherry says. I been pregnant since right around when I quit work.

Let me see him, Randy says.

Cherry holds him up in her arms just as I put a glass of whiskey in Randy's hands. He sips, steps closer to look at the baby.

Hmmph, he says, absently. He backs away. And I understand this, because I would have done the same thing myself a month ago.

Why didn't you say? he asks, stumbling as he tries to navigate his way to the door.

Insurance reasons, I say. Out on Breakneck, it's a good enough excuse for keeping any secret.

Randy looks confused.

Health insurance, I say. Cherry lost her job, I point out, hoping these random facts will add up to some kind of story in his head.

Oh, he says.

We sit around and try to make conversation, but my old buddy's in such a state with liquor there isn't much to talk about.

After he leaves Pauline pulls her mask off her face and says: County's got no right letting that boy drive for a living.

Next morning at dawn I swaddle the boy in old sweaters and a hat and scarf and rig him to my chest using an old backpack. I put a warm bottle in my hunting sack and we go into the swamp. It's a good day, too. We get three muskrat and locate a new den. I explain to the boy what we're looking for: bubble trails, mud under the ice. We set up a 110 Conibear, wire it up nice and steady. People don't know anymore that there's an art to trapping, but there is. A friend of mine from the clink said they're even eating raccoon and beaver up in Detroit now that the city's disappearing.

We're headed back to the house for lunch—the boy's cheeks are getting cold, the air picking up—when I feel someone else moving in the swamp. I still myself until I can hear the boy's breathing. I turn. There's someone at the far edge near the road, a figure in black. A man thrashing around, waving something in the air, walking a few feet, then crouching down to touch the ground.

Following the line of trees, I get closer. It's a shovel the man is waving. And the man is Randy. And right away I know what he's looking for. I realize I've known all along. And my knees almost buckle with the weight of it.

I turn and drop the rats and my traps and hold the boy close to my chest and run.

That bastard was looking for the boy, I tell Cherry. The boy's body, I say, swallowing and trying to catch my breath. I crane my neck around to look at the boy's face, as if the very mention of the result of another version of history is enough to turn back time, kill him.

Cherry opens her mouth wide and then covers it with her hands. She reaches out, unclips the clasps, and lifts Joey out of the backpack. She presses him to her chest, kisses his little head over and over.

There's only one way he would know to look there, I say. And what else would he be looking for?

No, she says.

I grab them both and pull them close to me. We're like one body, now.

We have to leave, I say. We have to leave Breakneck.

What? she says. Us? I can see the famous Cherry Jenkins rage machine about to turn crank and flare.

I've known Randy a long time, Cherry, and I'm telling you, something ain't right with him.

She says, He leaves a baby to die and we're the ones run out of town?

Except, we can't leave town because the Reliant's a wreck and I have to hit a few houses to afford to fix it and Pauline needs her prescriptions. By nightfall, we've started to doubt. Think it's a coincidence. Maybe Randy was out there after muskrat, we start to say. We have no choice. I can't get us out of there. And you know how when you're helpless you'll convince yourself you're crazy to think you need whatever you need? That's us. And though for the next five days I work through the night and Cherry pulls the drapes to peek out about four hundred times, we try to pretend it's all normal.

On the sixth day, Randy shows up, stomping his way onto the front porch, hauling some girl behind him. He's carrying a shotgun and he doesn't knock. They just walk into the kitchen while we're sitting there eating our corn flakes and toast. They stand in the entryway.

This here's Nadene, Randy says.

The girl is skinny and pale with dark circles around her eyes, the same eyes our boy has. She's got two ratty black braids tucked into her faded blue ski jacket. She can't be more than seventeen. She stares steadily but somewhat blankly at the boy, who's snuggled into Cherry's arms taking his after-breakfast snooze. I try to stay calm.

We know why they've come. But Randy's taking deep breaths, searching for the words to tell us, anyway. I wonder if it's hard for him because he really wants the boy back or because he just doesn't want to be the guy who ditched the boy in the first place.

Cherry draws herself tighter around the boy as if to say it'll be over her dead body that Randy will touch so much as one of our boy's toes. The whole world is coming to zero somewhere deep inside my chest. It's going to get really ugly if I don't find a way to make everyone happy.

Thing is, Randy says to me, I think you been lying to me.

He punctuates each word with a short, jerky wave of his shotgun, which he's holding by the base of the barrel. People out on Breakneck always think they need to have a gun in their hand to get their point across. I've never been one of those, so of course our gun is buried somewhere under the bed. Not even sure if it's loaded.

And I don't much care for liars, Randy continues, his whole enormous body waving back and forth as if in an invisible wind. He points his finger, clearly trying to think of what to say next.

The girl shoves him aside and he falls into the empty chair at our table. Sit down, R, she says. For Christ's sake.

Watch it, Cherry says, but the girl's got no idea it's about Christ. She thinks Cherry's getting up in her face so she immediately starts bobbing and weaving the way women do when they're in a fight. One of her braids falls out of her shirt. It's tied with a bit of yellow yarn.

That there baby you got. That baby's our'n, the girl says.

I'm thinking I remember seeing her face before. She's not the one I met at the Railway a year or so ago, the one I heard left Randy back in September. She looks like one of Con Waverly's daughters, the little girls who lived in a trailer off Breakneck about a mile out from the one I grew up in. Her jacket's too small, would maybe fit a child. Her wrists stick out, red from the cold.

I'm still trying to figure out what gentle thing to do, but Cherry's already had it, I can see, and she says in a low voice: You always in the habit of leaving your possessions on the side of the road?

The girl heaves a fast sigh and says, You don't know my life, okay? What it's like to be pregnant and not have nobody know! Don't you be all up in here judging me. She turns to Randy. See? she says, I knew they'd fucking leap to blaming!

At the sound of her screaming the boy starts to scream, too, and Randy leaps up out of his chair and shakes the gun at us. Fuck off! he says. It ain't your baby, so you got no right to say!

Well, I say, trying to sound reasonable, like a father talking to a teenager, Just about everybody might have something to say about this, Randy. Just about everybody. Probably the cops, too—

Don't you fucking threaten me, Joe! He reaches up around his collar and scratches at himself fiercely. Don't you go all townie on me, neither!

I know he's right: I shouldn't bring the cops into any of our business out here in the swamp. So I try to appeal to his sense of fairness. I say, He would have died if it wasn't for us.

Yeah, well he wouldn't exist if we didn't make him, the girl says smugly, drawing her lips back and flaring her nostrils.

I get up, slam the chair out of the way, and say, You fucking tried to kill him!

I see, out of the corner of my eye, Pauline raise her finger in warning. He's got a gun, her finger says. He's crazy, it says. She pulls her mask off her face and says to Randy, Would you and your girl like a cup of coffee? Piece of toast?

I see the girl sudden and quick eye the plate, purse her lips. And I stole that damned bread. But here's a reminder: there's always

Josie Sigler

somebody poorer than you.

I hold the plate out to her. Seriously, I say.

Cherry glares at both me and Pauline.

The girl eats the toast carefully, with her eyes on me, like I might take it back, or maybe laugh at her. I wonder how our boy managed to grow inside of her body, all angles and rags.

Randy's working up to say something, emitting a whole new series of grunts. He finally gets his shit together and says, I freaked, okay? I didn't know what to do and Nadene, the whole time she was screaming she didn't want it and then she was passed out and I just fucking freaked but I didn't mean to hurt it, Joe. I swear I didn't.

He says all of this, but he doesn't move to put his gun in the corner of the doorframe, which is how someone on Breakneck would say that he was mistaken, he was sorry, he's ready to negotiate without threats. Some kid down the way blew his foot off come tromping in a door where his dad was having a meeting that was going well.

Once back in grade school Randy and I went hunting for muskrat. We found one that had managed to swim its way out to the middle of the swamp with the trap on its leg. I hauled it in, nine years old and cursing Conibear's bullshit sudden kill advertising. But Randy, he laughed, shoved me aside. He tossed the thing out into the water to watch it swim frantically, dragging its cage to its death.

He and I negotiate, with that gun over his knees, what you might call a custody arrangement, similar to something the courts might cook up, similar to being Godparents, and Cherry cries the whole time because she thinks I'm dealing for real. Randy and I shake on it. Like my dad always said: Shake if you have to, but cross your fingers behind your back because the other guy's probably crossing his, too.

I look into Cherry's eyes, try to send her the message. I lift the boy from her arms. She sits totally stunned for a minute. Then she runs to the bedroom, screaming, Go to fucking hell! And that's pretty strong commentary from a woman like Cherry Jenkins.

I see Randy's finger tremble on the trigger.

I put the boy in the girl's arms. You know how to hold him? I ask, relaxing his neck into the crook of her arm.

She pouts when he starts to whimper, says, Got tons of little ones around my daddy's house. She looks down into his face. But he's the prettiest, she says. Ain't he?

I nod. My throat feels like someone's choking me.

They stand to go, and the terrible panic rises. I can't get a breath. I look at the boy, and I try to tell him with my eyes, too, that my promise is true. If there's anything I want my son to know, it's that there is such a thing as a no-fingers-crossed-real-deal between fathers and sons, a deal you strike and keep.

Will your wife be okay? Nadene asks.

She'll get used to it, I say.

But the fact is, she won't have to. Because that whole day while she's crying in the bed, I'm packing the Reliant, charging the battery. Soon as it's dark, I'm outside Randy's windows, looking for one unlocked or loose. When I find it, I let myself into the room where the girl sleeps. She's still wearing her jacket, her leg bent up on the mattress, her hair untied. I wish I had something more for the first mother of my son, but all I can do is slip fifty dollars in the back pocket of her jeans. I don't usually pray, but I say something like a prayer to her for what I'm taking. I know better than to think it's for her own good.

While I'm at it, I thank my dad for teaching me that if I ever needed to get lost fast, I-75 is a straight shot to the Florida Keys where it's awful hard to find a guy. I thank Pauline for suffering the cold air, for stroking Cherry's shoulder while they wait in the car down on Breakneck. I pray to Cherry because she never asks for more than I can give her.

But most of all, I'm praying to the boy. Because the first time he looked at me, he saw right into my bones. He saw everything about me, how once, after my father left, I punched my own mother in the mouth. He even saw how, for just a minute, I was going to leave him there on the side of the road and let him die, but I didn't. He let me want something better for all of us.

I creep through Randy's dark and stinking trailer to the living room where they've pushed a couch to the wall to make a crib. Randy sleeps nodding in a chair, guarding the boy, the gun across his knees. The boy's eyes are open in the dark and I can see them shining, like he's been there waiting for me, knowing I would come. He kicks his feet like he always does when I bend down to get him. I scoop him up in my arms. I stand there for a minute in the cold air just holding him to my chest. Then, we take the Breakneck Road, get the hell out of Dodge.

THE JOHNS
[*Chevelle Malibu*]

The johns waited outside the battered wooden doors, and because the breezeway was the only place to play once you outgrew the bathtub, some of them tried to make friends. A few even remembered your name. Before you understood this meant they were repeat customers, that felt smart. You could tell them apart by their belt buckles. Double-etched-star gave you candy, Copper Cactus cheered as you wobbled along the outside wall of the motel learning to stay up on your board, and Gold-Silver-Square shoved his hands deep into his pockets, looked at no one, said nothing with his kind and crooked mouth.

A passing-through john with an unremembered buckle was even there for your first tooth. Your hands behind your back, face tipped up to show just *how* loose and out it flew, a small blood-hollow Chiclet landing on the metal toe of his black boot.

He was embarrassed, and paid you.

That was what you understood first. The johns were embarrassed, and what they did was pay. They paid for your room, your dinner, your first skateboard and the ones that followed, your first leather, even the blinking pink sign over the interstate: *Girls, Girls, Girls*.

But you were the only girl. Most of the other dancing moms had boys, then, when you were still small. Maybe it was a coincidence. Or maybe most girls just don't survive that life, get sent to live with grandparents or aunts or fosters.

The boys were jealous because the johns always gave you more attention—and more cash. Once you got a fifty-dollar bill, crisp off the top of a stack clipped together. Besides, in any drought summer you were easily the best in the empty swimming pool, the board held to your feet like magic, your knuckles hardly bloody from scraping pavement. For you, gravity was a choice, not a requirement. You leapt over curbs and potholes in the wide desert night, the air dry as what you knew of love, a pocket full of change given by a stranger who wanted what your mom called *talking-time* but needed you gone to say whatever it was.

You slept cross-legged in the orange stuffed chair next to the scarred desk in the motel room you and your mom shared. She shook you awake, turned off the TV, and lifted you by the shoulders.

C'mon, she said.

But Ma, you said, your throat thick with sleep. *I* need talking-time.

C'mon, baby.

You stood up. Even at six or seven, you knew the drill.

She'd send you with Gloria, who said she'd watch you with the younger boys in the storage closet while she folded towels and sheets. But by the time you were ten years old you were a master at the art of escape, and Gloria knew better than anyone that a girl has to handle herself. Once the boys started wrestling or throwing rolls of toilet paper, it was easy enough to sneak out, walk past the johns for more loot and admiration, and back into the building. You hauled your board through the swinging metal doors to the kitchen where a new prep cook took up a mop and chased you out into the back alley, grunting through his clenched teeth, Chico Malo.

You stuck your tongue out. Couldn't he see that you had long hair under that baseball cap, for Christ's sake?

The bussers laughed at him, waved at you, and continued to practice their blackjack skills on an upturned milk crate, cigarettes clamped in their teeth.

In the big parking lot, the one that was good for speed but dangerous, eighteen-wheelers lined up like the beached whales you'd seen in a *National Geographic* some john left in the breezeway. But the only ocean you knew was the hot sea of asphalt that enveloped your body's continent. You turned, dropped your board, and coasted the smaller lot, jumping potholes and beer cans.

You passed the guys who stood in a tight circle at the back of the lot, waiting for the trailer-trash kids to hit them up for a baggie. Sometimes they thrust their chests out and strutted around, getting up in each other's faces. You weren't old enough to buy, so they looked right through you, except one guy, lanky with a long black ponytail, who smiled at you once or twice, touched the edge of his baseball cap. *Independent*, same brand as yours. You felt his eyes on you as you rolled past all the junk cars that Chester, owner of that fine palace, meant to fix but never had the time.

Black-ponytail, you thought, got it. Understood that you could float, you were a master of your trade. Looked like he might've topped a board in his day.

You tossed your board over the fence, hauled yourself to the other side, and headed to the Sunoco for grape gum, Butterfingers, Swedish Fish, chewy as tar, in a two-for-a-dollar plastic bag. Midnight was never so glorious as when you sat on the edge of the gas pump's island eating a whole bag of sour balls, one fluorescent shock after another until a thick rainbow grew in your throat.

On a good night, you'd get candy for the little boys waiting in the storage closet with Gloria. You did this to make up for being a girl, to make up for being between young and old. But most of your money, your mom's, too, went into the jar, the secret stash for your move to California, where your mom would do makeup for movie stars and you'd take on a real half-pipe. But until then, the gas station would have to do.

At midnight, when Mr. Al Adi left the station, he shooed you away from his handicap ramp, throwing his hands out as he yelled, Go home, pest-brat!

You laughed as he chased you, limping on his bad leg, through the parking lot.

Home! he yelled, pointing to the fence, to the lights rising from Chester's.

Of course all the Sand Niggers, as your mother called them, the Kitchen-Spics, as they called themselves, and the regular Indians, named such by Columbus, knew what it meant to have no home, to live in an America that has nothing to do with you, an America that would not believe your story. That America did not know the comfort of the stadium lights and the smell of gasoline and the one time it rained, washing the dust off everything and there you were: ripping through the oily puddles before they were sucked back into the dry earth. You could trace your name in that brief water even if no one knew your name, not even your teacher, who'd seen a hundred kids like you come and go.

Despite heat that boiled the marrow in your bones, summer was your best season. You stayed out late, your mom worked more, and that was money in the jar. But even better, summer meant no teachers. Teachers and guys like Mr. Al Adi hated all the motel kids, but especially your kind because they couldn't do anything about you or your situation. A person who considered himself some sort of upstanding citizen might talk big about busting Chester's to give you a decent Christian life, but it was easier to kid himself about exactly which services the dancers performed, to stay good with the neighbors in that nothing-town, interstate-town, where everyone was cheating in some way. Besides, even though it wasn't right, what your mom did, could he take the food right out of your mouth?

The ones who weren't righteous were just clueless, marveling that you came to school with your report cards unsigned and no separate pair of shoes for gym, either. Who cared about dodgeball, anyway, a sport designed out of nothing but meanness?

You preferred skill, grace, courage. You crooked your board on the lip of the gas island, hovering, grinding on the edge until Mr. Al Adi finally got his baseball bat and you sped into the darkness behind the station. You burst into the restroom where he would not look because he knew it was locked, had fixed that lock himself. He was also convinced he had scared you away for the night. You heard his car start. You stayed there next to the pissed-on toilet seat holding your nose until you could take it no more. You emerged just in time to see the taillights of his Coupe De Ville illuminating the ramp to the interstate.

You used the edge of the restroom floor to do a pretend drop-in.

When you skated to the front, your board wheelied, Adi Jr. was out for a smoke. He applauded your balance, the way you could let your board back down without a sound. Adi Jr. was always good audience for your latest trick. Plus, you were grateful that he kept breaking the lock on that restroom door. Not that he did it for your pleasure or anything. He broke the lock so he could hang out with his friends in the restroom when he was supposed to be working the graveyard shift.

Niiice, he said, as you Ollied over the metal circle where they delivered the gas. He applauded again, the fingers of his left hand gently tapping his right palm.

Gloria said Adi Jr. was a *maricon*. All it meant to you then was that he held his cigarette up high between drags and that he wanted to marry boys. This made you feel good about him because he'd never want to marry you. You'd heard enough to know you never wanted to be anyone's *wife*. Plus, it meant that Gloria sent you over for her Pepsi, never her sons, and told you to keep the change.

Adi Jr. was the only queer you knew. His face was smooth, like cream in coffee, and he would not give you a cigarette even when you begged. He did, however, take pity on you, letting you into the air-conditioning to steal candy if you didn't score. Sometimes, if you wore your hoodie with the big pocket, you could skife a roast beef sandwich and an Orange Crush, which was almost as good as orange juice, to surprise your mom with breakfast in bed.

Once Adi Jr.'s friends came, he ignored your tricks, and you made your way back home. You liked Adi Jr. You didn't want to cramp his style.

In the deepest part of night, after endless games of Mrs. Pacman with Devon, Jean's son, and the steak strips that someone always served up if you hung around long enough puppy-dogging, you knew it was time to go back to your room. Somehow, you managed to avoid returning too soon, and as you grew, this sixth sense grew also, so you could tell which john strolling through the breezeway clutching the front of his belt with both hands was your mom's last call. That was the second thing you understood about the johns: all they had to do was walk away when their time was up.

But your mother? She was still on duty. You came in, swinging your skateboard by one wheel. She was making up the bed with fresh sheets, opening the window for any hint of a breeze. She held her ratty old robe together with one hand and with the other tugged your ear for taking off on Gloria. She took you to the bathroom, wiped your face with a rough washcloth though you no longer needed help washing. She tucked you into the bed and put a firm kiss on your forehead.

You heard the slight rasping sound of her scrubbing her dance leotard in the sink, the clank of the metal hanger on the towel bar. She showered as you stretched the backs of your legs against the sheets, searching for a cool patch. You tried to stay awake long enough to feel her body curl behind yours, but you fell asleep to billows of steam pouring into the too-hot room.

In your morning, which was afternoon for most people, your mother seemed like more of a girl than you, thin because she smoked cigarettes while she walked you through the buffet. You ate piles of scrambled eggs like the yellow clouds of her hair. She listened to your jokes and buttered your toast and squeezed ketchup over your hash browns because she knew that was how you liked them.

After breakfast during a less-dry summer the two of you sat by the pool, you in cut-off shorts and a T-shirt, she in her bikini and an old button-up shirt left by a john, a guy so fat that it spilled out over his belt buckle, leaving him unremembered. Your mom ran her fingers through your limp and colorless hair. She untangled the fine snarls, sweet little pain you'll never forget. She tried to tie braids, which were supposed to keep you looking neat, but they always unraveled.

When she let you go, you jumped into the pool, trying to impress her, to hold her attention with your daring. She counted how many minutes you held your breath under the greenish water, counted back flips. Each time you emerged, you saw her skin-and-bone legs, her scarred arms, her tired face blurry in your chlorinated eyes. You saw everything about her, and she was yours.

She was yours until it was time to visit Chester for pay. Chester put his taxi hat on your head and let you beat him in arm wrestling. You allowed this only because you understood that he was part of the equation—if he paid your mom enough, you'd be on your way to California, where she could sit by the ocean instead of a dirty pool and you'd catch air all day. After Chester motorcycled your ragtaggle braids a few times, your mom begged a ride off Rhonda to get to the bank. You followed your mom as she wandered through the grocery store looking for food that didn't require cooking. And always, she bought a gallon of whole milk, which was stupid because it took up half the top shelf of the tiny fridge in your room.

It was your first-grade teacher who told her that without this milk you would end up in special ed or worse. So every night, while she painted her face and dressed herself in what seemed to you a bathing suit—sequined, silver and red, these were her colors—she fussed at you about choking down the plastic cup of slimy-sour thickness. If Jean or Rhonda came to the door to borrow some mascara or pantyhose, you tried to get away with pouring it down the toilet or drain.

You gotta drink it, she said when she caught you. You don't want to end up like Rusty. They don't get any milk on the Rez, and that's how come he's slow.

Rusty was the kid in 17. He was nine or ten and still playing with Legos in the bathtub while his mom talked with the johns. His legs were palsied and he'd probably never be able to get up on a board. But the milk was a lie, had nothing to do with Rusty being retarded. Even your mom knew that, probably. She just felt bad that she had to go dance and leave you alone in the room to watch TV, and even worse that you'd have to leave her alone later. It broke you both at once in different ways but only briefly because, as so-and-so said, what can't be cured must be endured, and it was your life. Your mother loved you. Nothing else mattered.

She loved you, anyway, when there was no special john. But whenever your mom met the nicest man, the john who was different from the rest in the breezeway, the john from away who might take you both away, too, there was less of her to go around.

He strode up to you and smiled. He shook your hand, or if he was really stupid, kissed it. He brought you a gift.

You were expected to entertain the special john by the pool. You had to be charming and sweet, do all the silly girl things you'd never officially learned. You'd watched enough TV to know that not everyone lived in a motel room, that for your mom to be happy you'd have to get a real house, and that a girl should be her father's little angel. These johns, as you understood it, were auditioning for fatherhood with your mother as director of the potential show. Back in the days when you wanted a TV family, wanted coffee tables and dishwashers and a separate bed for each person, back when you believed that it might actually happen, you honestly did try. You told knock-knock jokes and allowed yourself to be taken onto the special john's lap.

Thanks, man, you said, even if he gave you something babyish, something pink.

However, instead of sprouting wings and a halo when they pinched your cheek, you felt yourself wanting to chop off the thick-knuckled fingers that the special john then rested so casually on your mom's thigh or waist. Those fingers rubbed as if they were trying to dig up the stories under her skin.

She must look like her dad, said every special john eventually, as if he had just thought of it that minute. It meant you weren't pretty, that you did not have a cloud of curly blonde hair, soupy brown eyes, and long limbs like your mother.

But he was also asking who your father was, and you wondered, too. You both worried about the same thing: that your father was a john. He didn't even know you existed. You'd never be able to find him. Your reason for worry was obvious—where did the thick arch of your brow, the olive skin, the crooked mouth come from? The johns were thinking about child support, the possibility of shared custody, how you'd interrupt what they told your mom was romance but you knew, in the end, was always business.

Your mother never answered. She sure does love that new skateboard, don't she? your mom would reply as if you weren't standing right there.

Of course the special johns were the ones who bought you the most expensive presents, like the leather jacket you refused to take off for the entire summer after you turned twelve, sweat trickling from your armpits to your wrists. The thickness of leather covered the swell of your chest. With your new body came a new way. You stopped trying to please the johns. You took what they handed you and disappeared to fly through the big parking lot, playing chicken with the boys, tempting a truck to hit you, to take you out of the world before any john could fail to love you just because you weren't his.

Black-ponytail gave your jacket the thumbs up. You fishtailed a bit on your board to show your appreciation.

What's up, you said to Black-ponytail.

Yeah, he said, and once, Man, you busted that Anti-Casper.

You felt a connection. He was different from the others. He was like you. He didn't need some dad to support him. He made it without that shit. He took care of himself. He handed out the small baggies while his friends kept watch.

By then you knew that people who lived in a motel and sold themselves weren't going to end up with a TV family just because some john stayed a week and fought with Chester about who owned what and who owed what to whom. You surely didn't like the red-and-silver sequined suit, but you weren't sure, anymore, that you wanted your mom in the kitchen with an apron around her hips, either. Having a house might be overrated. Eating dinner at a table rather than on a broken air-conditioning unit probably would not really improve your life. It was just another way of getting bought by a man. And this was another thing you came to understand, possibly the only really important thing: a john would always be a john, even if he stayed. Though he never did.

And when he broke all his promises, when he got jealous, when he disappeared, leaving black eyes and fat lips in his wake, your mom took the night off. She used her makeup skills applying Cover Girl to hide her bruises. She put on a pair of jeans. She flipped the television on, pushed the milk at you, checked her watch while you dawdled drinking it. You both knew what she was going to do. No point discussing it. She would not look you in the eyes as she shoved you away from her at the door.

Stay, was all she said, as if you were a dog. You got school tomorrow.

You did not have to look in the jar to know it was empty. It didn't matter anyway. You thought of Jean, who slit her wrists in the bathtub, of retarded Rusty, who finally got carted away to live in a home, of Rhonda, who'd been at Chester's for twelve years—she'd probably get buried out back when she finally croaked with her legs in the air. California would always be in the next lifetime, and the cash for that lifetime got spent in a parking lot a hundred yards away.

You wished you still had the rollercoaster picture, your mom's hand gripping yours high above your heads as you screamed. If you had that picture, you could at least see her face, pretend that all terrors were the same, just your stomach dropping out, just the gravity you thought had no pull on you. But some fucking john stole that picture off the back of the toilet.

You paced. You tried not to imagine your mom in that bar on the edge of town, but you saw every moment of her night: her squeezing the lime, licking the salt. The bathroom stall. The flame blackening a metallic curve of spoon. This was how you learned to mix up hate and love and pity so well. You hated the cracked wall of the motel room and the stuck window and the stained sink. You hated the sour taste milk left in your mouth. You hated your mother so much your bones vibrated. Staring out the window, your hate was so pure it was the desert, and you followed it to the horizon, wanting to go over the edge of the earth.

But it was always light out there on the edge. You did not like how slippery it was, how fast it happened, the love you always came back to. You couldn't help it. You loved her wiry back, her cocked head when she was listening to you. God you loved her as you wanted her to love you.

Poor, poor you. If no one else was going to give you a decent dinner, you'd walk down to the restaurant and give yourself one. You'd come back to the room early, turn off the television and try to work on your reading. You'd put yourself to bed at a decent hour. And the sound of your sleep was the sound of the desert shifting into ocean, as it must, somewhere.

You woke to her retching in the toilet. You walked to her and knelt down, each time unsure of how to do what you must.

Sorry, sorry, she moaned.

It's okay. And you were so glad to have her body back, you meant it. How much? you asked. How much did you have?

Her red-snaked eyes rolled up and her shoulders shook. I dunno.

I jes' dunno, she mumbled. The reek of booze hit you full in the face.

You have to get it all out of there or they'll have to pump your stomach again, you said.

You were so cool, such a surgeon, as you cupped the back of her head in your palm, pinched the hollow of her cheeks to open her mouth. You pointed your trigger finger and pushed it into her throat. You felt the raised bumps on the back of her tongue, felt her whole body jolt as she finally spewed curdled liquor into the water. You washed your hands, unable to look at yourself in the streaked mirror. You filled a plastic cup with water and brought it to her cracked lips. You wiped the snot away. You helped her crawl to bed and pulled her shirt off and pushed her head and arms through one of your own.

You were the one whispering to her, then, the lie you shared: California, the long lashes of a starlet, the miles of sidewalk along the ocean where you would ride with the whales a safe distance from shore but just close enough to see the breath they left in the cool morning air.

Your mother slept, and you wished she'd sleep forever if that meant something besides dying, because after, she was a zombie for days. She crouched in a corner with her back against the wall. She wrapped her arms around her knees and rocked, crying, asking for her father like she didn't know he was dead.

You met your grandfather once, a silver-haired man with a UAW hat who would not let you and your mom in his screen door, not even for a cup of iced tea, like your grandmother, whose face was dimmed by the screen, suggested. You wished you remembered your grandma better, could have listened to the twang in her voice born of living in a place so far north, so cold. You wished you could have asked her who your mother had been before all of this. Who was the girl standing with her father in a photograph taped in the Gideon's Bible? What was it like to grow up where a girl could walk out miles into a lake, haze thick enough to swallow?

When your mom got that broken, Gloria was the only one she'd let come near her. Gloria soothed her in Spanish, laid a damp washcloth still smelling of bleach from the laundry on her head, and chastised her in a loving voice. Sweet bebe, you've got to stop doing this, now, and other such nonsense.

You were the sweet bebe who should go and get ready for school in Gloria's room where your mother did not have to see you.

Your mom never wanted you around, after. Maybe she did not want you to see her like that. Perhaps she thought you were mad. But then, perhaps you were just a reminder of her failure to score you the dad who was going to fix everything. And after several such failures, you decided to take matters into your own hands.

Skating the half-mile to the trailer park where you stood waiting for the bus with kids who were white trash but still better than you, you realized that your mom was too tired, too busy to get it right. You knew you didn't need a father. Ninety percent of the kids you stood with had no father. But maybe your mom did need a husband, a man to keep her on track, to keep her from putting everything in her arm.

As the school bus chugged and climbed the on-ramp, you realized your mom had been looking for the wrong things in a man, was all. She'd been looking for someone from away, a passer-through, a man who seemed like he had a nice house somewhere. You knew that if he did, it was probably full of wife and children. If he'd cheat on them, he'd cheat on you, too. Your mom had always landed the johns who were loud, who walked right up to you with a leather jacket instead of something reasonable, like a pack of gum and a Pepsi. She had always believed their romance, overlooking the johns who said nothing, offered nothing, told the truth about why they'd come. There was no such thing as love. But what the johns did to your mother in a dark motel room was the closest thing they could imagine.

You began your search on the weekends, hanging in the breezeway instead of at the Sunoco, although you missed shooting the shit with Adi Jr., who was applying to go to hairdresser school despite his father's insistence that he go to college to study engineering.

That is why America, Adi Jr. mimicked his father, tossing up his hands and limping across the room. You didn't make fun of Mr. Al Adi's limp anymore, not since Adi Jr. told you that his dad had stepped on a landmine as a kid and blown off half his leg. He wore a hollow one and had too much pride for a crutch. You felt, somehow, based on what they did not exactly say on TV, that your country, and thus you, were responsible for all bombs, all devastation. Worse, no one you knew benefited.

That's why America? Adi Jr. said. Bullshit. America so you can play with blonde-boy hair, he laughed. America because at least it ain't specifically legal to stone your faggot ass.

America, you thought, because anything was possible. Any past revisable. You zoomed back and forth over the pock-marked concrete just outside the dancers' motel-room doors, catching a little air here and there, slamming your trucks back down, until Rhonda opened her window and said, You're gonna have to scram, honey. She smiled, biting down on her lipstick-stained cigarette.

But you tucked your board under your arm, and kept right on chatting, flirting with the johns for the first time since you were little.

Of the four or five guys most often in the breezeway, you zeroed in on Gold-Silver-Square, a long-time customer whose face you were now tall enough to have memorized, right down to the grey eyes that never looked into yours. He was shy. He never gave presents. He never showed up drunk. He never fought with the other johns in the breezeway.

When you finally worked up the courage to say, Hey, all you got was a nod, his lower lip tucked over his upper teeth in an almost-smile. But that was something.

You learned, over the following weeks through painful extractions during which he kept his eyes to the sky and one side of his mouth turned down, that his name was Paul. Paul, so simple and kind-sounding. He lived in a trailer park off the next exit. He worked at the nuclear plant seven exits down. Excellent, you thought. He was a reasonable goal. You and your mom had about as much to offer him as he had to offer you. Plus, you could check on his truth. He could not lie. He was not passing-through.

I like it here, he said during your third conversation, in a rare burst of articulation. Work's good down at the plant and it ain't cold or nothin' like up north where I grew up. I's on the streets for awhile and there was no snow.

He strolled away, then, as if saying so many words had killed his urge for *talking-time* with your mom, but of course, you knew everything by then, knew that there was really no talking involved.

You began to watch for Paul night after night, and even during the day on weekends, which was when most of the repeat customers came. A good day was a day when your anticipation was satisfied by his appearance, his long bowed legs as he jumped out of his battered brown pickup truck and walked across the lot, his hands balled up in the pockets of the faded black jeans he always wore. A bad day was one on which you had misinterpreted his pattern, when he didn't show up, or you did not wait long enough and went over to the Sunoco where you endured Adi Jr.'s experiments on your lank and colorless locks. But on good days Paul leaned against the outside wall awaiting his turn with your mom and you skated back and forth, trying for the right ten seconds alone with him to say: *My mom really likes you. She likes you,* you'd say, looking up and down the breezeway conspiratorially, *better than any of these other guys.*

And though it had started out to be almost pretend, to be about pleasing your mom, you found over time that you really wanted him to take his hands out of his pockets, bend down, pull you into his at-first awkward arms, and squeeze you like a father would. You began to see signs that your mom really did prefer Paul over the other johns. As you got older, she was less cautious, and rarely did a john walk away without some kind of tag: *animal, user, freak.* But after Paul left, she'd just sit in the breezeway wrapped in her robe, damp from the shower, smoking a cigarette, shaking her head a bit, laughing. And once, after he had left and there were no other customers, you even slept in the bed without changing the sheets.

It was clear that Paul was secretly in love with your mom, too. He came back so often. He had to be the one who stole the rollercoaster photograph, just to keep it close, maybe on his bedside table while he dreamt, too, of the family you'd someday make. You examined your face in the mirror. You both had crooked mouths. You both had grey eyes, olive skin. And Paul, with his Gold-Silver-Square buckle, had been around as long as you could remember, maybe since before you were born, maybe since your mom was on the streets, which, from what you can figure, is when she got knocked up with you. Yes, Paul had been on those streets, then, perhaps.

Josie Sigler

Was he, finally, not just the solution to the problem at hand, but the real answer?

You're being a retard, Adi Jr. said when you told him. I mean, he said, flipping his waxed black bangs with his forefinger, Not to be a jerk, but those just ain't the rules, you know? A kid like you don't find her long lost pappy like in the movies or something.

But you were learning how good hope felt. You wanted to walk into the sunset between Paul and your mom. They'd both belong to you. You had not yet realized that women belong to men, and no one belongs to little girls. You had not yet broken the law of your sixth sense, and thus you had not yet been broken.

That afternoon in May—you had just turned thirteen—you slid your board down the long rail next to the stairs, passing the other kids, the stationary fools. You took the back way to Chester's, the roads past real houses where old ladies came out to gather the mail. You clipped a tube at a construction site after hours. You rode your board so fast you actually got goose bumps in your self-made wind. You rode for the sheer joy of it until the sun fell.

When you got home, Paul's truck was parked in the big lot. He was early. You grinned. You knew exactly who you were in that moment: none of the rules applied to you.

You flipped your board up into your hands and ran right through the breezeway, threw the door open. The room was dim, empty, silent, but the fresh smell of man, something like raw hamburger and Pine-sol, lingered. You felt that sudden pull in your chest, an ache you would later recognize as warning that something real was about to happen. And the girl part of you did not want to know, almost turned and walked out. But your eye's corner got caught in the framing golden light pouring from the bathroom door. The woman part of you stepped boldly into the room, turned toward that light. And there he was, the man you wanted as your father, the man who might have been your father, but could not be your father, now, could not be your father standing over your mother who lay in the bathtub, her legs spread, her sequined suit askew—

You won't even say what you saw. You wish you could not remember. You wish you could erase any night spangled with red and silver and the stained white porcelain of the tub and all belts undone and dangling over the sweet cantaloupe of human flesh waiting, waiting for love when all that was coming was goddamned acid, goddamned waste.

She looked, for just a second, with her wild-horse eyes, directly into you and she saw that her own life was true. She saw that she could never be your mother again.

No, she said, reaching up, shoving him away, trying to struggle up and out of the tub.

She stepped toward you, shaking. She wanted to hold you, you could tell. And lately, especially, you had started to want someone to hold you, had started to crave being held the way you used to crave sour balls, Swedish Fish. But you did not want her to touch you, not with her clothes all nasty, and not in front of this john, Gold-Silver-Square, who looked at you so coldly, as if you had walked into his urinal and interrupted God's business, as if you were nobody.

And you knew, then, that it was true. You were nobody. Your body was as hollow as Mr. Al Adi's leg. Your story was not about you. Nor was it about your mom. It was always about the johns, about them zipping up their pants, stepping over their own messes, tossing down a fifty, and walking out the door, through the breezeway, disappearing.

You ran then, ran away and toward the back lot in the blind dark. You looked over your shoulder to see your mom standing outside the door. She clutched a bed sheet over her body, sparkling and red. She looked like a gutted fish wrapped in butcher paper. Rhonda rushed to comfort her as she called your name again and again, her voice raw with terror.

Fuck her. You weren't going back there. You would run forever.

At the far edge of the lot, Black-ponytail was smoking a cigarette, leaning against the base of a stadium light that cast a fluorescent ring to the edges of his territory. His friends were nowhere in sight. He saluted you, but you did not pause. You did not want him to see you cry, see you lose your cool.

You needed Adi Jr. You needed to go and tell him he was right about everything, and that you were leaving, you could never come back. You threw yourself at the fence, sobbing, and began to climb, but

Black-ponytail caught your arm in his long fingers. You yanked away from him, slapped him. It felt so good that you dropped off the fence to punch at his arms, his bony chest. That was real, that sound of your fists against flesh.

What the fuck, he said. He bit his cigarette between his teeth and grabbed you and pressed you hard to him and you struggled.

Then you looked up at him, at his black-hole eyes, and said, Hold me. Hold me.

He relaxed his arms, threw his smoke down, and took your hand.

Okay, he said, shrugging. Okay.

You leaned into his thin body, wanting it to be your mom's body. And he was soft with you despite the shoulder blades that seemed to cut your hands. He smelled like onion and his last joint. You stood like that for what seemed like hours because you'd never been held by a man and it felt both horrible and safe. He led you to one of Chester's junk cars, a '67 Chevelle Malibu up on cinder blocks. You crawled into the back seat and he got in next to you, tossing off his hat.

Gloria had warned you about this, about getting into a car with a man. She said she got into a car with a man once down in Mexico and her whole life got lost. Anyone ever touches you here, or here, and she pointed. She said to bring your knee up, hard and fast.

But Black-ponytail talked to you. He told you about his first skateboard. He and his brothers made it themselves. They took the wheels off an old freezer that had killed his best friend's baby sister and nailed them onto a board. He talked on like that, soft, smooth. He talked until he took down his black hair that cascaded around you like a woman's, like a waterfall there in the desert and you thought you would drown.

Hands emerged from this waterfall and held your head. He kissed you, then, pressing you back on the seat. His tongue came snaking and full into your mouth and you tensed, turned your head away, crying again. So this was it. You felt his hardness against your belly, felt him fumbling with his belt buckle. He pried open your leather jacket.

With that opening, you felt something come up in you. It was the same feeling you had when you leapt on your board from the roof of the gas station restroom. You didn't even have to think about it. You just bailed when you saw you were going to break bones. Your heart began to pound not with fear but with realization: This was a man, and the johns were men, but this man was not your john. Then what were you? What did you have to be?

Stop, you said, pushing on his chest, closing your other hand around his windpipe. You got ready to pull your knee up hard and fast. Stop! you screamed.

And then, the only miracle you've ever known occurred. He stopped, moaned a laugh, and collapsed next to you on the seat, half of his body falling down onto the floor. He lifted himself up on one elbow and looked at you in the stream of bluish light that poured into the car.

He said, What are you, queer?

You didn't know if you were queer. You thought of Adi Jr., his face smooth, the smell of his cologne as he massaged your scalp. You thought of him hovering above the counter, ignoring that you had stolen a candy bar. You thought of how much he hurt when he loved.

Yeah, you said. I am.

Awwww, man, he said, tying his hair back. I thought so. What the fuck.

Sorry, you said, feeling yourself hit the ground without breaking bones. Just a few scrapes. You had defied other gravities, and you guessed this was one more.

He sat up. Guess it's watching your mom fuck all those losers, huh?

Of course he knew your mother, the junkie, the whore. He had been among those who had taken your California, dime by dime.

I gotta go, you said.

When you opened the door, there was Mr. Al Adi stepping from his Coupe De Ville with a baseball bat over his shoulder. Black-ponytail unfolded himself behind you, standing. Mr. Al Adi limped toward him, raising the bat in the air.

What are you doing? you said, out of breath.

Black-ponytail looked up and said, What the fuck?

Mr. Al Adi did not address either question. She's thirteen, he said. Thirteen!

He didn't do anything, you said.

I heard her scream, Mr. Al Adi said, lifting the bat even higher, dragging his leg as he prepared to brain Black-ponytail, ruin that pretty head.

Black-ponytail held both hands up and backed off, saying, I didn't touch her, man. I swear I didn't.

He turned fast and ran, his Chucks slapping the pavement long after he was out of the ring of light. You would not remember his name.

You turned to Mr. Al Adi, who was already limping back to his car.

Thank you, you said.

He paused, his face half in the light, half out.

It's not me you ought to thank, he said.

You walked through the parking lot, your feet strange on solid ground. You let yourself into your room. Your mom was asleep next to a bottle of vodka, her brow furrowed. You ran your finger along those lines to straighten them.

Later you would say to her:

But you laughed. I saw you laugh after Paul left, Ma.

She looked at you.

Jesus Christ, sweetheart, she said. You got two choices in this lifetime. You don't die laughing, you'll die crying.

You wanted a third way. You wanted to die flying, your feet on a board.

But there in the last room you'd ever share with her, you stumbled over your skateboard toward the little refrigerator. You got out the jug and poured. You sipped its sourness and nearly gagged. You walked to the bathroom and held the milk over the toilet. But then, you knew what it cost. You brought it to your lips. You swallowed. You swallowed the whole damned thing.

THE LAST TREES IN RIVER ROUGE WEEP FOR CARLOTTA CONTADINO
[*Galaxie*]

The men are coming to cut them down. To make another lot. And it's all because Jimmie Modesto's finally going to prison. Mr. Stryker, who owns our building, lost his son in Vietnam. He considers Jimmie a replacement ordered by God and was none too pleased to see him carted off in handcuffs. Mr. Stryker wants it done, wants the hoodlums out.

These trees were where I first saw Carlotta Contadino, her river-slate eyes peering around an elm during a game of hide and seek, her black ringlets falling to her waist. She smiled and alighted, avoiding capture. Her knockoff Keds were twin rabbits bounding away.

Carlotta says she doesn't remember that. Every kid from our neighborhood played back there, Shannon, for Christ's sake, she says. Besides, I couldn't have been more than ten.

But I'm sure the real reason she doesn't remember meeting me is that she saw not a girl, but a thin and tallish brush-cut boy peering through the trees.

When Jimmie Modesto and his crew met me in the vacant lot just beyond this grove of trees, they, too, mistook me for a boy. And I was glad. It was an honor to get your ass kicked by Jimmie Modesto. He and his buddies, infamous in our parts for vandalism and dope-smoking, hauled me into a dumpster filled with dirty baby diapers.

But I could have been any boy, then.

The spring he claimed Carlotta Contadino as his own, Jimmie came to recognize me as the boyish-girl who stood smoking Lucky Strikes at the edge of the thicket that flocked his lady love's building.

Carlotta was easily the most beautiful girl in the neighborhood. Every boy wanted her. Every boy knew she was a virgin. She was Catholic. And although it was 1985 and Michigan's very own Madonna had made it through the wilderness, Carlotta Contadino's Old World grandmother laid down the law at the purchasing of the first training bra: No boys allowed. Despite the fact that Carlotta went to public school, Gram made her wear regulation-length skirts. Of course, by her junior year, she curved in all the right places and wore turquoise fishnets under that ugly wool, details not lost on her admirers. Still, if Carlotta, sent on an errand to the 7-Eleven, lingered in the street an extra moment, perhaps tying her shoelaces, but perhaps talking to a boy, Gram Contadino appeared, her brow furrowed, on the stoop of Stryker's building to wave Carlotta in.

A boy's only real chance of winning her was to catch her walking home from school, which required dodging Mr. Stryker, who had taken to hosing down break-dancers and hoodlums. I got to watch many a drooling boy with a jambox on his shoulder and a well-devised plan fail as Carlotta strolled past laughing, shaking her head as a red-faced Mr. Stryker emerged from the side of the building and literally washed the boy out of Carlotta's hair.

Until Jimmie came along. He had the home-team advantage: Mr. Stryker had taken a liking to him ever since Jimmie offered to run to the store for the lottery ticket and a Slim Jim, just like Billy Stryker had done years ago. Jimmie had four years on the high school boys, had a man's body that trembled with muscle. He had a very convincing way of tipping his head to the side when he spoke. But most importantly, Jimmie had a copy of the confession schedule at Our Lady of Lourdes church. And he paid attention. On Fridays, Carlotta came home late, so Gram didn't always emerge in time to stop him. Having been forgiven her weekly sins, Carlotta was fresh to begin working on next week's list, the way Jimmie figured it. But Jimmie played it cool.

He bummed a cigarette from me, ducking between the side of the building and these trees. He cupped his long thin fingers around the flame I held and inhaled.

You're a good shit, he said absently, narrowing his eyes at the corner around which Carlotta would appear, shuffling through the first spent blossoms of spring. Jimmie moved casually but deftly to sit on the front stoop of our building, where he would try, as in a fairy tale, to achieve the kiss, the deed to Carlotta's territory, before Gram Contadino shooed him away with a rolled-up newspaper.

I stayed in the trees watching, feeling vaguely important, excited to have briefly entered the infamous Jimmie Modesto's ultra-cool world. I leaned my body's heat against the shade-cooled foundation, my feet tangled in roots that poked through the concrete. I finished my Lucky Strike as the falling light poured through the trees and into my own trunk.

&

But this grove of trees is not where the trouble began. Not exactly. Nor did Carlotta's life slide from safe to dangerous in a single moment there on the stoop with all the neighbors watching. The real trouble started on this balcony overlooking the trees, this balcony shielded from the neighborhood's view by the tallest branches.

Stryker's building used to be rowhouses for Ford's. Each of the twelve apartments has two rooms, plus a kitchen and bathroom. So if you get a balcony, too, you count yourself lucky. The apartment my uncle and I share is almost in the basement, and does not have a balcony. Gram Contadino's apartment, being on the second floor, does.

I became privy to their apartment when I started struggling in geometry in fall of sophomore year. I'm great in English, but that's where my brilliance ends. In a rare burst of parental concern, Uncle Manny said if my geometry grade fell below a C I had to quit my job at the gas station. Carlotta's sister Regina, who talked nonstop about going to Harvard, offered to tutor me. We studied at the Contadino's kitchen table because Uncle Manny works the night shift and needs the days quiet to sleep.

Regina spent most of our study time staring at me incredulously through her thick glasses as I toyed ignorantly with the shapes on the page before me. I don't see why you don't see how I got that, she said over the rattle of her grandmother making soup and the wheeze and occasional wailing alarm of Mr. Contadino's oxygen pump.

Mr. Contadino was crushed in an accident at Ford's. A year later, his wife left him, paralyzed and speechless, with two daughters to raise. The family moved in with Gram Contadino, who'd lived in Stryker's building *since God was a boy*, as she put it. Mr. Contadino was her only child, a rarity for Catholics, as I understood it. And thanks to great worker's comp, Mr. Contadino could afford to lie for the rest of his life on a hospital bed in what should have been the living room of Gram's apartment. His eyes, on occasion, blinked and glinted. The bedroom the three Contadino women shared was cluttered with the couches on which the girls slept, heaps of Carlotta's clothing, and piles of the old *New Yorker* magazines Regina collected.

This left the balcony for Jimmie Modesto's romancing.

While Regina and I figured the area of a dohectradon or whatever, Jimmie and Carlotta lay on a plastic lawn chair learning things far more interesting.

If it was a feat to win the girl, winning over Gram Contadino, who, over the course of a single summer, let him cross the threshold to sit with her precious gem on the balcony, the only private place in their home—of course that put Jimmie ever more squarely in the neighborhood hall of fame. Gram Contadino was no fool. She knew when she was beat, and it was clear Carlotta was head over heels. At least Jimmie was Catholic, Gram said. Jimmie was good to his mother. His dark eyes, ringed with thick black lashes, suggested he might rescue kittens from a burning house, despite the fact that he was, in Regina's assessment, *a punk*.

When Gram Contadino wasn't wandering out to offer him another Coke or cookie, Jimmie's mouth was on Carlotta's, sweeter than cookies and Coke no doubt. They made a game of it, seeing how far they could get every time Gram turned her back to chop a carrot. Jimmie's palms, and then his lips, found breasts popping out of the slinky halter top Carlotta wore beneath her Gram-approved cardigan.

Regina said, Boys don't marry girls who let them.

Skinny and pale, an incessant mouth-breather, Regina did not wear turquoise fishnets, did not attract the attention of boys. For different reasons, neither did I. And Regina saw us as aligned.

Aw, I said, it's not like they're doing it.

And of course the rejected hoodlums down in those trees were jealous as hell of exactly what Jimmie was doing. Not only had Jimmie cleaned himself up and gotten a job at Mitchell's Hardware, but he'd landed the hottest girl they knew. They twitched just to see him. They told every terrible joke.

How do you get an Italian girl pregnant? Come on the floor and let the flies do the rest.

Although half their mothers or grandmothers or great-grandmothers had once been Italian girls, they laughed as if this were the funniest thing they'd ever heard.

But Jimmie didn't care. He had a rose tattooed on his arm in honor of his own Italian mother, and he would marry an Italian girl. He was hoping for a job at the Ford Plant once the layoffs were over. He would buy a house in Trenton and Carlotta'd never want for a thing, or so he told her, those soft but certain whispered promise-words floating in through the screen door.

In the early evening, just as the trees began to glimmer in the fading sun, Gram Contadino said, Jimmie, you go home now, eh?

Jimmie seemed to oblige her instantly, strutting away from Carlotta in his jerking, bowlegged way. But then, he sat down in the folding chair at the foot of Mr. Contadino's bed. Kicking his long legs out, he leaned back, ran his hands through his greasy black hair, and chatted with Mr. Contadino as if he could respond.

Then this bastard mechanic forgets to reconnect the belt *and* he overcharges my mother by thirty dollars on top of this. Like we got money coming out our ears or gold mines in our basement. You want something done right, do it yourself. You know what I mean. . . .

After about ten minutes of this, Jimmie stood up, lightly punched Mr. Contadino on the shoulder, jutted his chin toward me in a gesture of smokers' solidarity, and went downstairs to watch the news with Mr. Stryker, just like Mr. Stryker's son had done in the evenings before he had the misfortune of pulling the pin of a faulty grenade just south of Hanoi.

Regina said that Jimmie was a mooch who ate Mr. Stryker's food, used Mr. Stryker's phone, and fell asleep on Mr. Stryker's couch. And Mr. Stryker covers him with a blanket, like Mr. Stryker's his mother or something, Regina said, staring at me intently and twisting one of her braids, which only turns Jimmie into a bigger and bigger mooch.

Jimmie isn't so bad, I said. Plus, your sister seems to like him. I smirked.

He does drugs, Regina said, opening her eyes wide and shaking her head, as if to say, *This is serious, you Neanderthal.*

Regina. You don't think half the guys in the neighborhood tried something or other? I raised my eyebrows at her. Not that I was Jimmie's biggest fan or anything, but I hadn't seen him stomping around the neighborhood tossing anyone into shitty dumpsters lately. If he was sleeping down at Mr. Stryker's, then he wasn't squatting in the small boarded-up house at the other end of the lot where half the guys he used to hang with stayed. And everyone knew Jimmie's dad was a drunk. Why shouldn't he stay at Mr. Stryker's?

He *does* do drugs, Regina said.

There is nothing you can do with people like Regina.

Once Jimmie left, Gram changed Mr. Contadino. She stomped a bit in her slippered feet, mumbling, I change his diapers back when, then I guess I change them now, hmm?

If Regina was done harping on my geometrical skills, I gave Gram Contadino a hand. I was strong and her son was heavy. After she suctioned his mouth, together we turned his carpish body, bones pushing against skin, mouth pursed desperately when Gram briefly disconnected his breathing tube. Unlike Jimmie, I did not look Mr. Contadino in the eyes as his mother and I spread a fresh white sheet over his withered but darkly forested legs. Gram Contadino hooked a bag of mush to her son's feeding tube, and turned to me.

You stay for supper? she asked.

I nodded briefly, as if I were the one doing her a favor, but all that waited for me downstairs was Uncle Manny's frozen chili or macaroni from a box.

At dinner I sat across from Carlotta, who, almost eighteen and a senior that year, did not concern herself with 'kids' like me and

Regina. On a particularly entertaining day, Carlotta might argue with Gram for the entire meal about whether she could or could not wear a certain off-the-shoulder blouse or tapered jeans. But usually, she stared at her *Cosmo*, which was fine. That way I could look at her without getting caught, could examine the gap between her front teeth, the green eye shadow on her eyelids, the slope of her shoulders still glowy from summer. She filed her nails and blew gently on the dust, holding her hand out to examine her work. She slurped her soup while Regina and Gram, having turned Mr. Contadino's television toward the table, watched *Jeopardy!*

&

Up to this point, my relations with the Contadinos were fairly benign, a word I learned the meaning of when the doctor said my mother's tumors were not. But one Sunday morning in late October a knock rattled our door. I answered to find Carlotta, who hadn't spoken two words to me since I had chased her through the trees in that long-ago game of hide-and-seek. I stood there in my pajama bottoms and my shirt from the gas station, my mouth open.

Can I help you? I said, trying not to wake Uncle Manny, who slept under the influence of his light blue pill and a martini on the sofa bed in our living room.

Hey, Carlotta said, leaning into the frame of the door a bit, gazing at Uncle Manny's thin form wrapped in the white sheet. I was taller than she was, so it felt like she was leaning right into my chest. Her hair smelled like rosemary.

Hey, I replied, blinking at her.

Um, listen. I'm not feeling that good this morning. . . .

That's too bad, I said, mystified.

And Regina is at a band camp thing. At this Carlotta rolled her eyes.

Yeah?

Do you think you could drive my grandma to church?

What? I ran my hand over my bedhead and stared. A long snore from Uncle Manny punctuated my confusion.

She repeated her question and added, My grandma really likes

THE LAST TREES IN RIVER ROUGE

you, so I thought. . . .

I gotta be stocking beer and pumping gas in like half an hour, I said. I pretended to be impatient when I actually felt exhilarated. Carlotta Contadino asking *me* for a favor.

Maybe, she suggested helpfully, squinting up at me and smiling with her glossed lips, you could call in sick.

And I did.

I had never been to church before because Uncle Manny isn't religious at all. He thinks religion, no matter what kind, is a scam, and did not even pray when my mother was dying. In fact, Uncle Manny is extra wary in general. He doesn't believe in the Space Program. And I don't mean he is politically opposed to it. He doesn't believe it actually exists. He says they filmed the moon landing in a TV studio in California.

I had also never driven that far before. Sometimes my boss, who thought I was sixteen, made me take cars around the back for a wash. If Gram Contadino, who knew perfectly well I was fifteen, noticed me swerving in Mr. Contadino's dented and rusty 1962 Galaxie, she didn't say anything. Perhaps she thought the Lord was more important than the law.

In the parking lot of Our Lady of Lourdes, I leapt from the car to open Gram's door. She smiled at me, her eyes sinking into her wrinkled face. She stood, smoothing her hands over her grey polyester suit, straightening the small flower she'd tucked into her lapel. She clutched my arm as we walked up the stairs of the church, where her friends *oohed* and *ahhed* at me. Beneath that arched door, my nose was stunned by sixteen shades of old lady perfume, not to mention the incense that wafted into the bright October day. It smelled a little like Carlotta's hair.

When this meeting was over, we went in and sat in a pew near the front. Of course, this was not the last time we'd sit. There was plenty of standing, sitting, and kneeling to go around. Gram Contadino gripped my forearm at each pose. Hauling her weight, plus that of her Bible, I'm sure I got a full aerobic workout. Gram Contadino sang out *hallelujah!* in my ear as I examined stained-glass windows, the walls ringed with terrible pictures plated in gold: Jesus Christ being nailed to his cross, his mother weeping, her tears tiny carved arcs. The statues of the Virgin Mary draped in robes, hands fisted beneath her chin or arms opened and bathed in candlelight. She had gotten such a bum rap. All the girls I knew would have shot themselves if they woke up one morning pregnant and had to explain to everyone that God did it.

At the offering of peace, the small old man next to me shook my hand. And then Gram Contadino smiled at me with the eyes that Carlotta inherited and said, quite humbly, Thank you, Shannon. I hate to miss.

When the mass ended, Gram Contadino said, sweet-breathed from the flat wafer of Christ's body, I usually stay for donuts and pinochle, but you get back to your life.

&

The malignancy started when I delivered Gram back home an hour before Carlotta expected her.

Holding Gram Contadino's heavy purse in the dank hallway of our building, I shoved my shoulder against the door. As it swung open, Jimmie Modesto appeared before me in nothing but his shorts. I sucked a sharp breath and he managed to slip behind the door just as Gram Contadino started to step in. I thanked my newfound God that she was watching her loafers to avoid catching them on the metal strip that was supposed to hold the carpet in place.

Carlotta emerged nude as Eve from the bedroom and covered her mouth with her hands. I had to think fast. The coffee I'd had for breakfast stank under my arms, stung my bladder.

Mr. Contadino, who seemed to watch from his bed, also seemed to know that his daughter was about to be caught. He made a choking noise. Before Gram could turn in his direction, I lifted her purse, tipped it and dumped its entire contents on the floor.

Gram jumped and turned her eyes down again, frowning.

Cripes, I said.

No need to take His name in vain, she said, bending down slowly toward the mess.

I rolled my eyes. Carlotta, before she ducked back into the

bedroom, smirked at her grandmother mostly for Jimmie's benefit. I could tell she was scared.

Kneeling at the edge of the door, I could see Jimmie on one side, zipping his pants as slowly and noiselessly as he could in rhythm with Mr. Contadino's heaving. If Gram caught Jimmie, he would never see Carlotta again, I was sure, let alone get naked with her. When he lifted his arms to pull his shirt on, I saw that he had gotten a second tattoo, still scabbed over, on his lower stomach. *Carlotta.* In cursive.

On the other side of the door, Gram's weathered hands collected pill bottles and inhalers and rosary beads and a small statue of the Virgin Mary. I pitied Gram, bent so and oblivious. She seemed old, used up, a joke. Despite the number of times I'd seen her grab Carlotta's chin and say: *I know what you do even when you don't say,* she did not know.

Carlotta emerged from the bedroom, clothed this time. She walked over and bent down to kiss her grandmother. She looked at me. We had to get Jimmie out of there.

I feel so bad about this, Gram, I said.

No problem, Shannon, she said, examining a broken snow globe whose water had leaked onto the floor. You'll be more careful next time.

No, really. I feel so bad that I'd like to take you to lunch, I said. I don't have any real family of my own except Uncle Manny, and you been so good about feeding me supper, and I'd like the company. We could go to McDonald's.

I guess Gram felt bad for me, either because of my familial woe or because I'd eat a burger that had been frozen for twenty years before some kid put it under a heating lamp. But, having missed a day's work, it was all I could afford to offer.

Okay, Shannon. If you want. You come, Carlie?

No, Grandma. I still don't feel good.

Great, I said, and took Gram quite firmly by the arm just as the wail of Mr. Contadino's oxygen pump lit the air. It was as if he'd done it on purpose.

Gram said, I have to suction, and pointed to her son, pulling away from me, her other arm sailing up two inches from Jimmie's hidden face.

Carlotta, who was bent gathering the small plastic children frozen for years in the fake winter of the snow globe, jumped up and said, I got it, Gram.

Gram shrugged her shoulders and turned to take my arm. Jimmie smiled at me and exaggerated the wiping of sweat from his brow. Carlotta elbowed me and mouthed *Smooth*.

And I was taken into their fold.

Later that afternoon, my stomach paying for my good deed, I walked Gram upstairs a second time. Jimmie waited outside the door, his hair combed down and his hands folded in front of him like the perfect altar boy.

You come to visit Carlie, Gram Contadino said, nodding at him.

Yeah, Jimmie said, I mean, yes, Ma'am. He tilted his head to the side, checking Gram's face to see if during our trip to strip mall heaven I had revealed his secret. But I hadn't.

We entered the living room. Gram moved immediately to suction Mr. Contadino, who responded with a low moan.

And Jimmie Modesto, king of River Rouge, pulled me by the elbow toward the balcony, saying, Whyn'tcha have a Coke with us?

I've heard that at death a movie of your life passes before you. In each life, I'm sure there are only a few scenes worthwhile, a few that make the cut. I swear to you, the first time I walked onto this balcony I felt my life change. The entire future that stretched out before me jumped and bent and zigzagged to another conclusion. I looked to the right, and to the left, and saw that the three of us were completely enclosed by pines. Oaks. A maple tree. Our trees.

We drank Cokes. Jimmie laughed about their close call. He slapped my back about fifty times, like I had won *The Price Is Right* or something. He talked about being on the waiting list at Ford's and how he would marry Carlotta and wasn't it cool I was in on it? Jimmie jiggled his legs, watching the clock as often as his girl, who leaned silently against the rungs of the balcony, surreptitiously smoking a Lucky Strike. She had blown her cover. Carlotta, having risked the dark temper of her grandmother and her reputation, too, had now incurred the risk of trusting me. And we both knew she owed me one, showing up at my door with that phony story.

At dark, Gram shouted, Time for Jimmie to go!

See you tomorrow? Carlotta asked him.

Nah, baby. I gotta go to the hardware store and tomorrow's Devil's Night, he said. He wiggled his eyebrows at me, but I said nothing. I hated Devil's Night, when, inevitably, neighborhood assholes who likely used to be dear friends to Jimmie toilet-papered these sacred trees, upsetting Mr. Stryker, who then haunted the trees for weeks, making it impossible to share a smoke or get some peace down there without him calling the cops.

I wish you wouldn't go, Carlotta whined.

I gotta have some kind of fun before I sign my life away, huh?

I stood at the same time as Jimmie and he took a step back so I could pass into the apartment that smelled of garlic and butter. Carlotta and Jimmie kissed goodbye behind me.

Gram came in and grabbed my chin. You stop smoking, Shannon, she said.

Yeah, I said, having no such intention.

Mr. Contadino's breathing machine let out a long sigh, perhaps his version of lamenting the day's events, as Jimmie stood before him babbling about a cousin who'd cut his finger at Ford's and *the bastards that wouldn't even give him worker's comp.* Mr. Contadino was lucky they hadn't been *bastards like that back in the day.*

After Jimmie had finally gone, Carlotta came over to me, put her hand on my arm, and said, Thank you. Her eyes were wet and bright, as if she'd cry.

It's no problem, I said.

We aren't *actually*–

I don't need details, I said.

I love him, she whispered fiercely, gripping my arm tighter.

Okay, I said, but Carlotta grabbed my other arm.

I love him, she said again.

She pulled me toward her until I could feel her breath on my face, see the green of her eye shadow shimmering.

Regina, lugging her tuba, opened the door just in time to see

Carlotta clinging to me. Regina opened her mouth, but then shut it, and put the tuba down. It didn't take much to get on Regina's bad side, and I imagined once you were there, only riches and prayers could get you out. She picked up one of her beloved *New Yorkers* and pointedly walked into the bedroom, where she stayed through dinner.

And I stayed that night even after Gram planted her rough kisses on our cheeks and went to bed. I stood to head downstairs. But Carlotta grabbed me, spun me back around. She picked up a deck of playing cards from the table.

Dare you, she said, to beat me at Slap Jack.

So began our tradition of sitting around in the kitchen late at night eating leftovers, sneaking wine from Gram's special nighttime bottle, playing easy card games. Carlotta was fast and competitive and hooted whenever she managed to slap the jack, howled when I was faster. The skin on the back of my hand stung with the red print of her fingers. I won three times in a row. Carlotta shoved me out of my chair and fell onto me, cracking up.

Regina appeared in the doorway. You guys are loud, she said, cutting her eyes. This only made us laugh harder. In a way I felt sorry being mean to Regina. But it felt good to be in on any joke with the fabulous Carlotta Contadino, even if the joke was mean.

&

The next Saturday Regina and I were scheduled to work on my ever-worsening geometry. She kept her voice like a razor the whole time, making sure I knew she was offended by my presence. After an hour, I bailed, saying I was tired. I walked out to the balcony where Carlotta sat waiting for Jimmie, shivering, her feet propped up on the railing. It was supposed to snow.

I glanced inside to be sure Gram wasn't watching before I lit a smoke and handed it to her.

Good thing you're here, she said, leaning forward in her chair to cuff my leg.

Yeah, I said.

As she exhaled, she said,

Just then Jimmie appeared, creeping up through the woods beneath the balcony.

Hey, he whispered, and jerked his head toward the street. I got a surprise. Come on.

Carlotta told Gram she and I were going to the early movie at the dollar cinema.

Why not Regina? Gram asked.

Regina has to study.

And you don't have to study? Gram asked, but she relented.

Regina followed us to the lot where Carlotta and I snuck into a ruined and absolutely glorious baby blue '67 Thunderbird Jimmie had borrowed.

Jimmie came up behind Regina and tugged first one braid, and when she turned her head, the other. He laughed, but she glared at me.

You're going to fail geometry, Regina said to me. Or worse.

But the frigid breeze from the open window and the speed blew the sweet rosemary of Carlotta's hair into my face. Who could care about geometry given this alternative?

We rode to Luna Pier Beach. Less than an hour from the River Rouge where rust fell from the sky, a different world existed, blue and golden and perfect. We had the place to ourselves.

Too cold for tourists, Jimmie said, yanking a sandwich out of the bag Gram had packed for Carlotta and me—she never sent us anywhere without food—and eating it in about three bites. He drew a bottle of whiskey out of his jacket and passed it to Carlotta, who sipped off of it, made a sour face, and passed it to me.

To get warmed up, she said, shuddering, standing, running toward the water.

I put the bottle to my mouth, aware that it had touched hers. The bitter burn raced from my lips to my stomach. Jimmie and I watched as Carlotta danced and cartwheeled at the edge of the water.

She's a piece, ain't she? Jimmie said, but I didn't answer. I couldn't. I was too busy watching Carlotta as she twisted and turned into the wind, her hair the tail of a wild pony.

Jimmie dug around in his jean jacket and held up a small baggie filled with white powder, which he tucked into his pinky fingernail. He held it out to me. So Regina was right.

Want a bump?

I shrugged, trying to act like this was a common occurrence, being offered crank. Not today.

Suit yourself. I ain't slept, he said, and pressed his nose, sucking up the powder. He shook his head and tucked the baggie quickly away as Carlotta flopped down between us.

We sat shoulder to shoulder as the sun went down. Jimmie wrapped his jacket around her. Carlotta took a chug from the whiskey bottle, hugging it even as we raced back to River Rouge so we wouldn't miss curfew. Besides, Jimmie had to *take care of business.*

Jimmie pulled the car onto the curb in front of our building, leapt out to press Carlotta against the passenger door. The whiskey bottle clunked against metal as he kissed and kissed her. He let her go just as winter's first snow began to fall.

Jesus, Jimmie, she said, pulling her shoulder to her mouth to wipe it.

That's right. Jesus and me. We're brothers, he said.

Take care of her, he said to me, grabbing the whiskey, twisting off the cap and sipping as he walked backward to the driver's side.

I nodded. The tiny confetti of snowflakes caught in Carlotta's hair.

I don't need to be taken care of, Carlotta said smartly.

Jimmie threw out his hands and said, Then what am I working so fuckin' hard for?

He sped off. I unlocked the front door and walked a laughing Carlotta up to her apartment. She fumbled for her key, but she couldn't seem to grasp it. I bent over and plucked it from her warm pocket. I opened the door to the sound of Mr. Contadino's oxygen pump. His dulled eyes flashed in the brief light from the hallway.

I'm thirsty, Carlotta said, so I walked her to the kitchen, poured a glass of orange juice. I was jonesing for a smoke something fierce. I let myself out to the balcony.

I heard Carlotta suctioning Mr. Contadino so he would not go into a spasm, setting off the alarm, waking Gram and Regina up.

I worried about her sticking that tube into his throat while she was drunk, but I was even more anxious that he'd tell on us, ruining what was looking like another late night of talking, smoking, and playing gin rummy.

Carlotta emerged, still wearing her slippers. She stole my cigarette, smoked with one hand and drank orange juice with the other. She was quiet. I could tell she was thinking hard. Snow fell and clung to the barren branches of these trees. I lit another cigarette.

Finally she said, So I love Jimmie. I pretty much loved him since I can remember. I used to see him walking around in the lot, and I couldn't take my eyes off him.

Yeah, I said, wondering what she was getting at.

Well, what about you? You never talk about, like, who you're into. Who do you . . .

I shrugged. I'm just busy, I said, spewing a cloud of smoke into the cold air.

She tilted her head and raised her eyebrows.

He's no one you know, I added. He was no one I knew, either.

Have you ever even kissed a boy? she asked.

I paused. I hated it when Carlotta made fun of me. But I couldn't lie. I shook my head, and then tossed my smoke over the side of the balcony to indicate I was done with the topic.

But she persisted. Never been kissed, hmmmm? she said. She put her own cigarette under her slipper, crushing it so the slight smell of burnt rubber filled the air.

Whatever, I said.

C'mere, she said, and reached toward me.

I wanted to pull away. To pretend I didn't understand. But the fact is, I let Carlotta Contadino, Jimmie Modesto's girl, tip my head to the side, take my shoulders in her hands, and put her mouth on mine. Her breath was smoke and oranges and whiskey. I tried to play it cool, chin up a bit, hands in my pockets. But she leaned into me. She pushed her arms up the back of my jacket and wound herself around me. She kept on kissing until I melted—until it felt like the thin plate of bone that covered my heart would snap—and I slid my arms around her.

It was supposed to be an experiment. A favor. But Carlotta pulled away, gasping. Remember those moments I told you about? The ones when everything changes so you can never go back, and when you die, they'll play again before you? Well, despite my Catholicism being kind of newfangled, while I looked into Carlotta's eyes, I said a brief prayer that the film would get caught on repeat in that moment, that I could play it over and over until the end of time, us standing on this balcony in each other's arms.

But who can ever leave it there? I pushed her back on the plastic chair covered with snow. I laid myself on top of her. Sirens wailed in the empty lot beyond these trees, but we didn't hear them.

Regina, of course, did. And as I grabbed the handle of the door on my way out that night, I felt a hand on my shoulder. I turned to find her leering at me, her retainered grin metallically demonic in the near-dawn dimness of the room.

Pervert, she said. I saw you.

I shoved her hand away and grabbed her by her flannel pajama shirt. Fuck you, Regina.

I saw you, she repeated, lisping.

You keep your fucking mouth shut, I said, trying to sound like a thug, like a man, like Jimmie, but my voice shook.

Regina smirked and yanked herself away.

I didn't sleep much that night. I got out of bed just after dawn for a smoke. Standing at the edge of the building I heard Gram greet Mr. Stryker, who was likely brushing snow off the stoop. I heard Mr. Stryker tell Gram that the cops had busted a group of guys in the condemned house at the edge of the lot, hauled them off to jail in the middle of the night.

Good riddance, he said. Hoodlums.

My heart pounded. What about Jimmie?

The whole morning at the gas station I planned what I would do, how I would care for Carlotta, who would clearly be destroyed if Jimmie was arrested.

But around noon Jimmie's car pulled into the station, and he got out, apparently unharmed.

I leapt up from the counter where I had been reading the news, and ran out to pump his gas. I couldn't tell what was worse, having made out with his girl, or having worried about him all morning like I was his girl.

All Jimmie said was, I was safe as a baby at Stryker's by the time it all went down. I get out while the getting's good.

That was good advice for me, too. But I found myself right back on this balcony, Carlotta's hand in mine.

&

On top of all of this, Uncle Manny was giving me all kinds of crap for becoming Catholic. See, every few weeks, Jimmie had a Sunday off and Carlotta faked some cramps and I took Regina and Gram Contadino to church. Regina, who took every opportunity to look at me and mouth *pervert*, could have gone it alone, I suppose, but I encouraged long games of pinochle (really, are there any other kind?) and multiple donuts and stopped for lunch afterward. This gave blessed Jimmie enough time to zip up his jeans effectively, to get down to the woods for a smoke, which we shared, usually, upon my return from church.

You're a good shit, Shannon, Jimmie said. His trade line. But he liked me. Trusted me.

Gonna go in and get some sleep? I asked.

Nah, I gotta meet a buddy.

Jimmie, I said. Maybe you should cut it out.

He shrugged and said, Selling hardware don't pay.

But Jimmie, I said. What about Ford's?

Ha, he said.

And Jimmie, his eyes bloodshot and his hand shaking on his smoke, wandered through the trees to the edge of the lot where he'd cut another deal.

&

On Thanksgiving I sat in the back bedroom after dinner sipping off Jimmie's flask and painting Carlotta's dainty toenails. Carlotta hummed along to Madonna's *Like A Virgin*, which she wasn't anymore, which was partly my fault, and for more reasons than I cared to count.

She babbled about some outfit in a magazine over the blare of the football game Gram had turned on for a drooling Mr. Contadino in the living room.

I'm going to move to L.A. and be a fashion designer, she said.

Like hell you are, Jimmie said, without taking his eyes off the game he watched from the doorway. I ain't moving to freaking California, he said.

Who said you were invited? Carlotta said, tossing her magazine to the floor.

Come on, you guys, I said. They had been at each other's throats the entire week.

My point is, Jimmie said, you ain't.

Screw you, Jimmie, Carlotta retorted.

If I get lucky, you just might, he said, and walked out. For once, Carlotta did not follow him down to Mr. Stryker's, begging him for forgiveness. But that night, after everyone had gone to bed, Carlotta followed me downstairs, and there in my twin bed I knelt before her, pushed up her grey wool skirt, took down her panties, and found another robed Madonna. Fumbling, nervous, and thankful for the ten thousand jokes I'd heard that told me what I should do, I kissed her there again and again.

And early in the morning, after Carlotta had snuck back upstairs, I dropped by Mr. Stryker's on my way to work to see if Jimmie was okay. Of course I knew more about why he shouldn't be okay than he did, and that was why I had to ask.

Jimmie answered the door with the phone tucked between his shoulder and chin. I walked in and watched as he jotted notes on an old pay stub.

You got it. I'll be there, he said into the phone, and hung up.

What? he said to me.

Where's Mr. Stryker? I asked.

Running the snowblower, he said.

I paused. Then I asked, You alright? I mean, with Carlotta.

Whatever, he said. I got bigger fish to fry.

Like what?

Jimmie grinned. Like never mind, he said. And then he punched me in the arm. That is, he said, unless you wanna get in on this shit tonight.

No thanks, I said. I have to study for the damned geometry exam.

You want me to hook you up? he asked, and if he had, maybe I would have passed the exam, but Mr. Stryker appeared in the door, and I shook my head.

Mr. Stryker put his hands on his lower back and grunted in pain. He said, Jimmie, will you take the snowblower to the storage room?

Jimmie said, Sure thing. Then he said to me, Wanna help?

I nodded.

You all are good kids, Mr. Stryker said, and handed Jimmie his keys.

Jimmie carried the blower and I carried the hose down to the basement. Jimmie unlocked the door to the storage room to reveal at least twenty stacked boxes: Televisions, VCRs, stereos.

What the fuck, Jimmie, I said.

Nobody but me ever comes down here, he grinned. Check it out, he said. And he opened the thin drawer of Mr. Stryker's tool table and pointed. In it were baggies filled with white powder and weed.

You sure I can't hook you up? he said.

Maybe later, I said, and walked up the stairs and into the frigid air outside. I walked to the gas station kicking myself the whole time. Now that I knew about his stash, there was no other way to see it: Jimmie and I were in it together.

&

The day after Christmas break began Carlotta spent the night at my house again. We lay together as a cold slice of air poured in from the window. I began to kiss her, to take off her clothes as I had become accustomed to doing. As I reached to unbutton her jeans, her best tapered pair, she grabbed both of my hands.

Stop, she said.

She curled into the crook of my arm and lay there for a long time. She was shaking. I thought she knew I was going to tell her I loved her. But when she lifted her head I saw that mascara had dripped down her cheeks like sooty rain. I took her chin in my hand.

What's wrong? I asked.

The air seemed to buzz around her as she told me the words I guessed in the hairsplit second before she said them.

I'm pregnant.

I tried to keep cool. How pregnant?

At least a month. Maybe two.

I didn't know what to say, so I sat there like a brick for about a minute, then, stuttering, asked the formal question. What are you going to do?

She said, I'm going to get rid of it.

What? I said, jerking my head back to look at her.

I turn eighteen in three weeks.

But—but— I stuttered.

She sat up, pulled her hair back, wiped her face.

What, she said. Don't look at me like that. You know Jimmie can't raise it. And I can't have a baby alone.

Jimmie can straighten his shit up, Carlotta. Just tell him.

Jimmie knows, she said. Jimmie's going to pay for it.

For some reason, this hit me in the gut, made me feel the first vague stirrings of a real hate for Jimmie. I could be thankful that it wasn't mine, I supposed, that it couldn't be mine, that there were no consequences to our kind of loving. At least that was what I imagined at the time. But there are always consequences for loving someone as much as I loved Carlotta.

The fact was, it felt like the baby was mine.

&

Christmas Eve, I went to the Contadino's for dinner, since, as usual, Uncle Manny was sleeping, having worked the night shift, and I had promised Gram I would drive her to Midnight Mass. In their apartment the television blared A Christmas Carol and Regina and Gram clattered plates as they prepared dinner. I picked up Mr. Contadino's suction tube to clear out his mouth, but just as I pried his lips open someone knocked on the door.

I answered to find Jimmie, who put his hands on my shoulders and hauled me out. You're probably thinking it's almost a condition of mine, this opening doors to find malignancies on the other side. Jimmie's breath was rank and his hands were shaking as he bounced up and down on the balls of his feet. He wore a grease-stained T-shirt with a giant rip and his shoes were untied. I was convinced this was it, the end of me. He must have seen us behind the dumpster the day before or stealing a quick kiss on the steps the day before that.

But Jimmie wasn't trying to kill me.

Thank God it was you who answered the door, he said, talking like someone had hit his fast-forward button. Thank God, I mean. I went out with the guys last night—we lifted. We lifted some shit. This is a bad time. A bad time for me to fuck up. These guys are going to kick my ass if I show up in the lot. I'm so fucked.

No shit, I said. He was a wreck.

They got a warrant out, he said.

Christ, Jimmie, I said.

How the fuck else you think I'm gonna take care of shit? He said, pleading. Help me. You gotta tell her. I can't. And I need someplace to go.

You can't go to Stryker's?

Yeah, right, said Jimmie, picking at his face. I pulled his hand away. I heard the thin wail of Mr. Contadino's pump through the wall and the commotion of the three women inside to get to him, save him from drowning.

I quickly led Jimmie down the stairs, out the door. I hid him between the trees and the building, near my bedroom window.

Stay right here, I said, as if Jimmie were a toddler prone to wandering off.

I went into our apartment and tiptoed up to Uncle Manny's bedside table. I paused a moment, but then picked up the pack of Lucky Strikes to tap it against my palm, knocking two to the floor. I picked them up. Uncle Manny slept on, so I took a pill bottle, opened it, and extracted a light blue pill. In the kitchen, I poured a glass of water. I carried my loot to the bedroom, opened the window and hauled Jimmie in, shushing him all the while. I sat him down on the bed. Like a small child, Jimmie lifted his arms and let me strip his shirt from his body. I pulled a white T from my drawer and together, we pulled it over his shoulders, wider than mine. I put the pill on his tongue and handed him the water. He drank it, and turned on his side in my bed.

I climbed out my window, ran around the front of the building, unlocked the door, ran up the stairs, and burst into the Contadino's apartment.

Where were you? Carlotta asked.

Out of breath, I said, Jimmie was at the door. His mom is sick. Walked him down to his car. Doesn't look like he'll make it to dinner.

Gram said, Too bad, Jimmie.

Regina snorted.

Carlotta merely turned and went into the bedroom. She threw herself down on her couch and buried her face in the pillow. I followed and closed the door behind us.

Tell me, she said. And I did.

Where is he? she asked, lifting her face to look at me.

Downstairs in my bed.

Christ! she said. What are we going to do?

I shrugged, ran my hand through my hair, smelled my own nervous sweat.

We'll figure it out in the morning, I said. He's gotta sleep it off some before he can decide what to do.

What about tonight?

We eat dinner like nothing's wrong.

Okay, Carlotta said. She stood before the cracked mirror and opened her mouth to put on her mascara. When she was through, I pulled her into my arms.

It will be okay, I said.

But when I opened the door to leave, Regina nearly fell into the room.

Hey perverts, she greeted us. So, she said, are you going to call the police, or am I?

Fucking Regina.

Carlotta's voice came from behind me. I am, she said.

I was torn, I have to admit. There was a part of me that didn't want Jimmie caught, didn't want the police crawling around our neighborhood deciding who could stay and who was too much trouble. I tried to sit on the couch, but my leg wouldn't stop jiggling. I tried to suction Mr. Contadino, accidentally setting off his alarm. Regina was too busy being glad she'd finally won to help me. Carlotta was apparently unable to move.

Gram came running from the kitchen. She re-attached the tube to the sensor, and the alarm went silent just as the sirens began to blip outside, that short pulse the cops do when they think they've got an easy arrest on their hands.

Gram walked to the window. Lights in the street, she said.

Yeah, Regina said.

What? Gram asked. Who in our building?

Carlotta said, It's Jimmie, Grandma.

Not our Jimmie, Gram said.

Poor Gram.

Let's go watch, said Regina. And I hated her in that moment more than I ever had and more than I ever would again.

Carlotta grabbed her coat. She walked toward the door, but then turned back to Mr. Contadino and stood before him. She leaned over and held him pressed to her chest.

I'm scared, she said.

Of course Mr. Contadino did not move.

The four of us made our way down the stairs in time to see Uncle Manny answer the door in his shorts. He blinked at the two cops standing before him.

We have a warrant for the arrest of a James Modesto, the burly cop said.

Who's James Modesto? Uncle Manny said.

The cops pushed past Uncle Manny and Regina said, Back bedroom to the right.

Uncle Manny wiped his face with his palm. There's a boy in your room? he asked.

No, I said. Well, yes, I corrected myself. It's a friend of Carlotta's. I took Carlotta's hand in mine.

Uncle Manny stared at our hands and shook his head like he had a spider in his ear. I was in for it.

Mr. Stryker emerged from his apartment just in time to hear the cops reading a groggy Jimmie his rights. They shoved him into the hallway, his hands cuffed behind his back. My T-shirt was tight across his chest and his nose bled onto the white front.

Why? Mr. Stryker asked. Why Jimmie?

And of course it was Regina who piped up. He's been dealing.

Mr. Stryker raised his eyebrows. But why? he asked, clearly unable to believe that his precious Jimmie, his son in spirit, would do such a thing.

Regina looked into Gram's face and supplied the answer, To pay for an abortion.

Jimmie sneered at Regina.

Gram put her hand to Carlotta's shoulder. No, she said. Not with Jimmie.

Yes, Gram, Carlotta said. Yes.

And with Shannon, too, Regina said.

What? said Uncle Manny. What?

I stood straight up. I looked at each of them in turn, and then Carlotta, and then at Carlotta's stomach, at the baby, not even a bulge yet.

It's true, I said. And it was. It was the truest thing.

Uncle Manny said, So you aren't with that boy?

No, I said.

I could see he was relieved, that he just wanted to go back to bed, that my hand in Carlotta's had not really registered.

But it had registered with Jimmie. He woke right up. As the cop pushed the back of his head to get him to walk through the door he said, I'll kill you.

And I said to Mr. Stryker, Might want to give the cops the key to your storage unit.

I'll fucking kill you, Jimmie shouted, and lunged at me. The taller cop elbowed him in the face, and Jimmie fell, writhing, as the other cop tugged at his ankles, headed for the door.

No, Mr. Stryker said as they dragged Jimmie down the steps. No.

&

Gram still wanted to go to Midnight Mass, and I felt the least I could do was offer to take her. She accepted, but was silent in the car. I tried to find the right words, but there are no right words for *I'm in love with your granddaughter.* It was so much more than sex. How could I tell Gram that?

Throughout the service Gram stayed curled on her knees, praying. Already familiar with the sit-and-stand routines, I followed along, but every time I looked up at the enormous crucifix, at the blood dripping from Jesus' palms, I felt like I was going to throw up. And every time I looked at the Holy Virgin bowing her head toward me from the altar's side, I felt like I would cry. Something else happened, though, as the priest intoned the words, *Blessed art thou among women and blessed is the fruit of thy womb.* I closed my eyes. I begged something inside of myself to be strong, to stick with this life no matter what happened. *The Lord is with thee.* I reached out for Gram's hand, feeling the beads of her rosary trapped between her fingers. I squeezed her hand. She did not squeeze back, but she did not take her hand away. Every once in awhile God does you a little favor, gives you a gift so small that you believe things will be okay.

When we got home Mr. Stryker was sitting on the stoop in the dark, his face in his hands. He looked at Gram and said, Right under my nose. Right under my nose. He threw his arm out toward the last trees, the vacant lot. Then he put his face to Gram's breasts and cried— big heavy man sobs that clung to the air. And I am sure it was in that moment that he made his decision. To cut down everything. To clear everything. All of this.

And later, crying in my own arms, Carlotta made her choice, too. To hold on. To keep what precious little we could from that year of our lives.

&

It's spring again, almost Easter, and Carlotta's belly is round and heavy. Jimmie's getting ten years. And the men are here. They're cutting down the last of our childhood and the noise of this breaking is terrible. I guess it's not much of a loss, really, to anyone else. But I'm dreaming on this balcony while the trees weep. I'm dreaming that Jimmie doesn't get paroled, that he lets me live if he does. I'm dreaming that Regina gets into Harvard and moves far away. I'm dreaming of a house in Trenton, of a family who lives in a house with trees in the front yard, trees a boy could climb.

It's not what will happen, of course. I couldn't even pass geometry. But it's what Carlotta and I talk about in the evenings before Gram Contadino sends me home.

EVEN THE CROCUSES
[Impala]

Spring came in with a rain so steady even the crocuses drowned. The baby kept his croup despite Marcy's trip to the free clinic four towns away. Then, John got stuck with the long route, Indianapolis to Omaha, and would spend even more time in the cab of an eighteen-wheeler, making it just that much harder for Marcy to do what she must: stop loving Walt.

Down on his luck. That was all John had told Marcy. *An old friend down on his luck.* His brow was creased, sincere, almost stupid. He held Linnie and Ronny, one on each knee, Jake at his feet. Now that they had a house of their own, John said, they should do a good turn for a friend. People had certainly done right by them, offering spare rooms and basements as they moved from Michigan to Ohio to Illinois to Indiana while John was out of work.

Okay, Marcy said, worn out, as always, by her husband's goodness.

The next week, Walt moved into their basement, and all winter his tall body filled the doorways. He leaned into Marcy, put his hand to her lower back while John was driving across the wide Indiana night. Walt stood with Marcy in the melting backyard once the sun had gone down. They clicked the necks of their beer bottles. Then Walt left, carrying his green duffel bag. He slammed the screen door so the sound of wounded metal echoed through the house.

Marcy dialed Paula, tucking the phone between her chin and shoulder to wash a pile of dishes slick with chicken fat. She looked out the window at Paula's house, a small ranch with scuffed peach siding. Paula's pale face hovered in her kitchen window. Marcy could see the dark circles beneath Paula's eyes, even from across the driveway that separated their houses.

Paula listened until Marcy was through crying about the things she could cry about, which did not include Walt. Paula promised again in her dry-crackled voice, Bad stuff in threes.

Yeah, Marcy agreed, but she was thinking of Walt, his washboard stomach in a white wifebeater, the smell left in his jeans when she picked them up off the basement floor.

Maybe so, she repeated. Threes.

Perhaps the rain did not count, was just the season.

Then Paula talked about her ex-husband, child support, and her son, who was captain of the football team. But Marcy was not listening. What if the rain did count? If there was a fourth bad thing, could there be a fifth? Could it go on and on?

Two days later the basement cat gave birth to another litter of kittens. One was born dead, a caul covering the blue face opened in a silent yowl.

Linnie wept, turning her face against John's flannel shirt as he lowered the kitten, wrapped in a plastic bag, into the soggy ground. Marcy, her lanky hair lifting on the breeze, stood a few feet away holding the baby. Ronny clung to her waist. If Marcy hadn't had a sip or two of whiskey, if she hadn't been thinking of Walt, she might have noticed Ronny poking at his scalp, rubbing his head like a dog against the waistband of her jeans.

At the end of April, while her husband slept in the cab of his truck two states away, Marcy ruined the Impala on her way home from the bar where she'd been looking for Walt, who'd taken her arm and squeezed it until he left marks, who'd left her, who'd slammed the door.

Worse, Linnie had seen.

They never should have let him in. Marcy should have realized. Stopped herself. But that wasn't the way it worked with Walt. Only hours after he yelled so loud she could feel the mean warmth of his breath, Marcy pressed her fingers to her arm and felt a sharp ache rise up in her skin that had nothing to do with the bruises. She couldn't stand the empty rooms, the hallways where she had pushed herself up against him. The afternoon hours when the kids watched TV, Tom chasing Jerry over and over again.

That afternoon, Marcy asked Paula to stay with the kids. She drove to the bar where she did not find Walt. She did not find him and knew he was in bed with someone else. She did not find him, did not find him, and each time she did not she swallowed another shot.

Paula stood wide-mouthed on Marcy's front porch the next morning at dawn as Marcy emerged, drunk, from the car she'd driven over the curb and into the telephone pole shared by the two houses. Of course, Paula gathered Marcy up, called her daughter Carla to look after the kids, walked Marcy to her house, and talked to the police as only a woman in a town so small can do.

You leave her be, Paula told the young officer who'd taken the call. She pushed the breathalyzer away from Marcy's face. Girl's not drunk, can't you see? She's got three babies and her man's on the road. Poor girl's tired, is all.

He wrinkled his brow and looked at the chief, who shook his head slightly, quick. No one should call Paula Humphrees—a woman who had lost everything and yet managed to live with herself, feed her children, and mop her floors—a liar.

The young officer gave up. He called the tow truck himself.

Lady fell asleep behind the wheel, he said. Exhaustion.

No, Marcy wanted to scream. She wasn't tired. And it wasn't John she missed. It was Walt. He had said he could do whatever the hell he pleased on a Friday night. He had slammed the door. He had taken his green duffel bag. Everything Walt owned fit in that bag, so he had no reason to come back to her. She leaned against Paula's shoulder and wept because she could not say any of this.

John'll be home soon. John will come home, she cried.

Paula held her out at arm's length and said, You got a good man in John. He knows what you're up against. You straighten yourself out. You just take care of those kids and keep your attitude up and it'll all come out in the wash, Paula said, nodding her head toward Marcy quickly and genuinely with each syllable.

I hope so, Marcy said. Then she threw up on Paula's kitchen floor.

But after a cup of coffee and a shower, Marcy did feel a streak of hope run through her chest as she walked across her yard in borrowed clothes. She straightened her spine. She would keep her promises. She would take the baby from Carla's arms, apologize. She would smile at Linnie and Ronny, who expected her to love them as she had before she stopped loving their father. And later, she would welcome her husband into her arms and serve spaghetti for supper despite the fact that it seemed she would fall down at any moment, shout out all her secrets, leave a stain of red sauce on the floor.

But she didn't fall down. She stayed sober for three days.

Then, that Wednesday, walking through the kitchen, she felt a drop of water fall on the back of her neck.

Figures, she said, and lit a Kool.

In the driveway slick with oily puddles that dripped their rainbowed messages into the street, John worked on the car, trying to get it running before he left again. This time for ten days. According to him, Marcy had merely *loosened the guts* of the car and he might be able *to wire the strut with a coat hanger.* That was John. Bury. Work. Fix. Fish. Leave. Drive. Play with Linnie and Ronny. Leave streaks on the floor. Work more. Never a question about where she went for hours in the late afternoon, why she returned with twigs and leaves in her hair.

But wrecking the car, he'd said, was the last straw. He didn't know what her problem was, but she had to *shape up. Lay off the booze.* Still, he had kissed her cheek. Had said all of it with such immense faith, as if he knew she could and would do what he asked.

She tried Walt again. Despite the many messages Marcy left at the convenience store where he worked, he hadn't called her back. And the manager would not give her any information, would not even say if he had seen Walt. She settled the phone back on the receiver.

Putting her hand out to catch a drop of water from the ceiling, Marcy thought of Walt's hands, larger than John's, warm on her back. She opened the cupboard and poured herself a shot of whiskey. Just a small one.

She put a pan on the floor under the leak and looked at the clock. It was three, and the kids would be home soon. She had laundry to fold. Dinner to make.

Jake wailed, woken from his nap by John starting the Impala. Marcy gathered him from the kids' bedroom and returned to the kitchen table. He sniffled on her lap as she lit another cigarette. Holding it in her teeth, she dipped her finger into the whiskey and rubbed it on Jake's gums where he was cutting molars. Paula'd taught her that trick. Marcy drank the whiskey down, feeling the burn in her chest that blotted out everything except the kitten crawling up her jeans with its needle-sharp claws.

Linnie and Ronny came in the door just in time to see her fling the kitten off her leg. It hit the refrigerator with a thud, fell to the floor, and staggered into the quickly filling pan of water, which sloshed onto the tile, seeping into the grey places where the shellac had worn off. The kitten leapt back up, ready to fight.

Linnie, a fine mist from the steady light drizzle in her mousy hair, put her bag down on the table, picked up the kitten, and patted him as if trying to set an example for the proper treatment of animals. She stared first at the ceiling and then at the pan on the floor. With all the authority a third-grader could muster, she raised her eyebrows at her mother, and ran immediately to tell her father, her footprints coming up brown and wet in the dead grass.

Linnie knelt down next to John, put her head beneath the car and presumably began speaking in the breathless newsy voice Marcy knew well. Then John heaved a sigh Marcy could see even from the screen door where she stood with Ronny, who pushed his tongue into the gap in the front of his mouth, scratched his head.

John slid out from beneath the Impala and walked toward them, a smear of grease on his forehead, mud on his jeans, his slightness doubled when he hunched his shoulders. Marcy shifted away and turned her face aside as he entered and looked up at the roof that had succumbed to the pressure of too many spring storms.

We'll fix it up, he said, smiling at each of the children, winking. And then, Stop scratching yourself, son, at which Ronny tucked his hands in his pockets. John reached into his own pocket for his hanky and wiped the thick snot that rested on Jake's upper lip. Marcy felt John's eyes on the side of her turned face.

The kids steadied a ladder and he climbed up and stapled thick plastic over the hole.

It's a slow enough leak. Should hold until I get back, John said, taking one of Marcy's smokes, lighting it, cringing at the menthol.

John said goodbye to them that evening on the front porch. He jogged across the yard in the fading light, the small brown suitcase with his clothes banging against his thigh.

Linnie and Ronny ran after him and Linnie caught his hand. I want you to stay, Linnie said, as she always did.

Marcy rolled her eyes as John set his suitcase down and picked Linnie up to hug her before he got into his little Dart.

I'll be back on Tuesday, he said, kissing each of the two older children one more time through the rolled-down window. Marcy felt him trying to catch her eye, get her to promise again, *no booze*. But she kept looking at the baby, and John had nothing left to do but drive away.

Why did they always leave? It had started with Marcy's father going out every Saturday night, gambling until dawn, coming home to place bill after bill in her hand, to say, *that's what a grand feels like.* Then, he took it out of her hand and disappeared for a week. And her brother, after punching her father and then the wall, had walked out the door without looking back, without remembering that she was his pet, his special girl. And then John, driving, driving on the flat expanse of highway as the sun dropped to the horizon, that red light spreading flat in a line and then disappearing.

In the house, Marcy straddled Jake to give him his medicine. She forced his mouth open and pushed the pink goo in just to watch him spit it back out. Jake was thinner and smaller at almost a year old than Linnie or Ronny had been.

Paula said Jake would grow when he grew.

Leave it be, she said. *Doctors'll say anything to get your business. How you think they cured croup on the frontier?*

Marcy gave up on the medicine. She put Jake in his playpen,

settled Linnie and Ronnie in front of the TV, and shut herself in the small bedroom. She plugged in the phone and sat on the pullout sofa bed. Dialing, she crossed her fingers as the phone began to ring.

When the manager answered, she asked for Walt.

He's not here, said the manager, and hung up, not even asking for her message.

Marcy pressed her fingers to her mouth, feeling the familiar urge rise. She crawled under the pullout bed, stuck her arm up into the empty space where the bed fit when it was folded in, and grabbed a bottle. She held it in her lap for a long time.

She'd promised John. If nothing else, she had to at least cut down. Instead of five swallows, maybe four, then three, and so on. The way you went on a diet or quit smoking. Tuesday was still six whole days away.

When she left the bedroom, she found Jake in his high chair with a cracker. Linnie stood at the stove holding a package of macaroni and cheese. The water was already boiling. Ronny played with toy trucks under the table, pretending to radio his father. He emerged, saying, Linnie, I need a glass of milk.

Marcy stepped between Linnie and the stove, taking the package, saying, I got it.

Sorry, said Linnie.

Marcy, as she juggled the glass of milk and the box of macaroni, wanted to smack her daughter for knowing, for seeing her.

Marcy and Linnie ate without talking while Ronny sang *The Gambler* and Jake added his wordless babble. After dinner, they settled in front of the television.

Linnie, Ronny asked, Will you scratch my head?

Linnie shifted her slim body on the couch to welcome her brother, and she rubbed the top of his head with her fingertips. Marcy watched, a quiet awful hunger in her chest. Who needed Marcy besides the baby? Besides Walt?

Long after the two kids were in bed, Marcy sat at the kitchen table holding Jake in one arm, her other hand on the phone. Jake's thick breath was a comfort, and she rubbed her lips along his forehead at the hairline. After making love, she and Walt used to bring the baby into bed with them. Marcy had pretended then that Jake was Walt's son.

In the mornings, she listened to Paula's voice prattle on.

Paula said she'd heard on the news that the Mississinewa dam was ready to bust because the river was pushing so hard. The rain continued through the afternoons and water the color of urine pooled into the plastic stapled over the kitchen ceiling.

Marcy straddled Jake three times a day and Jake spat the medicine out.

She called the convenience store.

She kept to her plan. At least during the day, that is, she didn't drink more than one at a time. She sipped from a glass of rum and Coke in the evenings, and rum and coffee in the morning. She was never actually drunk like she had been when she crashed the car. At least when she was alone with Jake during the days, she was mostly sober.

The kids came home from school with a letter saying that lice was going around. The words blurred as she read them. She ran her hands over the children's heads, glancing down between important moments on *The Cosby Show*. The roots of her daughter's hair seemed to squirm. Were those bugs? No. Dandruff. Fuzz from her sweatshirt.

You're fine, she said to Linnie.

The phone rang, and she shooed them into the living room, thinking it might be Walt. Hello, she said softly.

Telemarketer.

Paula came for coffee. She held Ronny on her lap. She looked down at the crown of Ronny's head and said, You better shampoo this one, Marce. Look here, she said.

Marcy nodded. Her own head pounded and a constant elevator of nausea moved between her throat and her gut. It wasn't fair. She was barely drinking.

I'll take care of it, Marcy said, and Paula continued to drink her coffee politely, holding her head high on her shoulders, away from Ronny.

The cat wound around Marcy's legs and cried because they were out of cat food.

She needs to feed her babies, Linnie said, and Paula squinted at Marcy.

Are you okay? Paula asked.

Fine, said Marcy. We're on our way to the store right now.

Paula pursed her lips. Can I drive you? she asked.

No, thank you, said Marcy. She heard her voice sounding official, as if she were talking to someone at church, the bank, her mother.

She sent Paula home, strapped the kids into the wired-up Impala and went to Save More where they bought cat food and more macaroni.

Coming up the front steps carrying Jake and the groceries she stumbled. Jake wailed. Half an hour later, she spilled the macaroni into the sink. She dropped a lit cigarette in her lap. She lay down on the couch and let Linnie take Jake to bed.

In the middle of that night, she woke. She checked on each of her babies. Then she sat on the couch and wept and clawed at her head. She could have killed them.

May came. And it kept raining.

It had been over a month since she'd seen Walt and it would be two more days before he called, crying, at seven in the morning, asking Marcy to pick him up at the bus station in Indianapolis. A sweet heaviness coursed through her belly at the sound of his voice.

She rushed the kids onto the school bus and ran inside to wash her hair while Jake cried in his playpen.

Within twenty minutes, she was standing on Paula's porch holding Jake out, asking for an hour. She could see what Paula was thinking: it was always more than an hour. And the last time, of course, Marcy had been gone all night, drinking and then dancing with a man who wasn't her husband, which by now, of course, had gotten around. It would have been even worse if Paula had known that Marcy had a lover, too, and the man she had rubbed herself against wasn't even him. Just a warm body moving to the music piped out from the jukebox. A warm body'd do Paula some good now and then, Marcy thought.

But she didn't say any of this. She appealed to Paula by acting as if she were there on business. She heard that official tone come into her voice again. Our tenant needs a ride. Marcy explained that Walt was stranded. I don't want to take the baby to the bus station all the way out in Indianapolis.

Paula relented.

Marcy sped on the highway all the way to the low grey station where Walt sat on the curb, his long legs bent high, a cigarette hanging from his mouth. Marcy pulled up beside him. She got out of the car prepared to act like they always did in public. Like strangers. But when Walt rose and held his arms open, she moved into them, inhaling the animal smell of his chest. He cried into her hair, I'm sorry. I need you, Marce.

When they got back into the car, he said, Let's get out of here. Let's go somewhere no one knows us.

The rain had stopped for what seemed the first time in weeks, and the air pressed on Marcy, filled her hungry lungs.

The next twelve hours would be a blur to Marcy later. She and Walt drove out to the edge of the farm where Walt used to work, found an empty field to lie in. Walt pulled a bottle of vodka and a joint from his duffel.

The kids get off the bus in a few hours, Marcy said.

You got some time for me, first? Walt said, already getting that edge in his voice.

Marcy nodded, leaned back, let him kiss her, let him put the bottle to her mouth so that an hour later her children had been pushed all the way to the edges of her mind, the edges where things were not quite real, and certainly time did not pass that quickly, certainly it was not dark and cold on the damp blanket when Marcy woke to the rich iron smell of the earth turning over for spring, a light rain falling again.

She sat up. She nudged a naked Walt, who merely said, Humphh.

Get up, she hissed.

They pulled their wet clothes back on and folded the smell of their sex in the blanket. Marcy sped home, swerving on the wet roads.

When they arrived, Paula was at Marcy's house. She was asleep and drooling on the couch, a *TV Guide* on her chest, a bandana tied over her head. Marcy shooed Walt to the basement, ran her hands through her tangled hair, and nudged Paula on the shoulder. She woke with a start and looked around blearily, but then she quickly sat up, pulled her sweater over her shoulders.

The kids are asleep, Paula said as she buttoned her sweater. They need their heads washed, too, Marcy, she added. Marcy saw Paula was trying to keep cool, but just like it had been with Marcy's mother, a vein in Paula's forehead bulged, letting Marcy know she was a disappointment.

Her voice was slurred, and she made an effort to steady it, to speak the ends of words as she explained, I'm sorry, Paula, but the bus came in late and then we had to run some err—

It's none of my business, Paula said.

Paula, I— Marcy began, but stopped herself. What could she say? Thank you. Tears came to her eyes.

Paula softened a bit. Look. I got an idea of the story here, and all I'm gonna say is this. That Walt's no good for these babies. You got a man who stays around, puts food on the table.

Marcy nodded, but opened her mouth and lied, Nothing's going on with Walt.

You want my opinion, you ask him to go.

Marcy nodded again, leaning forward to cry against Paula's sleeve. They could both smell the sick sweet smell of her drunken breath. They could both hear Walt banging around in the basement and cursing.

You need to shampoo them kids, Paula repeated. No way around it.

I'm just so tired, Marcy said.

I'll call in the morning, ok? Paula said as she stepped out onto the front porch, her greying hair caught briefly in the porch light.

Marcy opened the basement door and whistled down to Walt, who crept up on hands and knees. They curled up in the bed Marcy used to share with her husband.

In the morning, she woke Linnie and Ronny and said brightly, Uncle Walt is back.

He's not my uncle, Linnie said, turning toward the wall.

Ronny sucked his thumb, itched at his ear.

Marcy lifted Jake, whose diaper was soaking. She laid him on the changing table.

Go out to the kitchen and I'll make you pancakes before school, she told Linnie and Ronny.

Linnie turned at the door and said, The nurse said we can't come back to school.

Marcy turned, holding the wet diaper.

What?

She made us sit in the office all day. She called and called, but there was no answer, Linnie said, her voice rising.

Marcy walked over to Linnie and glanced down at her head. She ran her hand over the head once, twice. She glanced at Ronny, who was itching his neck. Nonsense. Marcy did not have time for this.

Gripping her daughter by the shoulders, she leaned forward. You're going to school, she said dully into Linnie's face.

Linnie screamed then. She ran from the room and down the hall.

Marcy swept the baby into her arms. She ran after Linnie, who had reached the kitchen. Marcy was slow compared to Linnie, who was wiry and fast. By the time Marcy put the baby on the floor, Linnie already had the phone in her hand, red plastic cord dragging the base behind. She jumped to reach the top of the refrigerator where John had left an emergency number.

No, said Marcy, out of breath, pulling her daughter to the floor.

Linnie struggled, beginning to cry in earnest, which made Ronny cry, and Jake chimed in, his face open and wet, double the snot of the last weeks dripping onto his shirt front.

Ronny tried to drag his mother from his sister.

Marcy pulled the phone from Linnie's hands and put the receiver back on the hook. Her daughter struggled to get the phone back. She sank her teeth into Marcy's arm. Marcy yelped and dropped the phone to push at her daughter's face.

Walt appeared at the door in his briefs, his hair on end, eyes bloodshot, a cigarette dangling from his mouth. What the fuck, he said, picking up a diaperless Jake in one arm and pulling Ronny toward him. Walt was so tall his head bumped against the full and heavy plastic John had stapled over the hole.

The phone rang. Linnie yanked it from her mother, answered it, sobbing, Daddy?

But it was Paula Humphrees's voice that came, distant and tinny, through the receiver. Over the crying boys, Marcy heard her ask, What's wrong, sweetie? Linnie?

By the time Marcy wrestled the phone away from Linnie again, Paula was already walking through the yard. She let herself in. Marcy watched from atop Linnie as Paula let her eyes move up and down Walt's body, thin, white, hairy, old track marks on the arms and between the fingers.

Now Linnie was chanting senselessly, Where were you, where were you, where—

Linnie! Paula said sharply.

Linnie stopped, and curled into a ball, clasping her knees with her arms. She rocked back and forth on her bottom.

What's going on here? Paula asked.

I'd sure like to know, said Walt, unashamed, preening his chest hair.

Paula glared at him.

Marcy stood, brushed her hands down the front of her nightgown and said, not to Paula but to Walt, School nurse says Linnie's got a case of lice, which she ain't, and she's upset.

Paula pulled Ronny away from Walt, who handed her Jake, too, and disappeared from the room, his face grim. Great, Marcy thought. Now he would leave again.

Paula put the baby in his high chair and Ronny in a chair and said, Come here, Linnie. Linnie lifted her body from the floor and sat in the chair next to Ronny.

Paula pulled Marcy over by the arm and said, Look.

She lifted a lock of Linnie's hair to reveal clusters of small waxy nits clinging to the strands, small grey bugs moving in the white line of scalp.

And look here, she said.

She held both sides of Ronny's head and tilted it into the light, which caught the fresh blood in his scratches.

Marcy gagged. She heard the door slam and the Impala start and peel out of the driveway.

Seems like I'll be running to the store for you, Paula said staunchly.

Still, as she walked from the kitchen, she chucked Linnie under the chin, gently pinched one of the baby's toes. She turned around and said to Linnie, It will be over with by tonight as long as we do it right.

Marcy could see the relief in her daughter's shoulders as Linnie hunched over the table and rested her head in her arms. They sat in silence together for a few moments. Linnie lifted her head briefly and reached out to crush Walt's cigarette butt still smoking in the ashtray.

Linnie looked at Marcy then and said, It's his fault.

Marcy pulled Linnie from her chair and stood before her.

It is, Linnie said.

Marcy brought her right hand up as if swearing a quick oath. She paused for only a second before bringing it down on Linnie's cheek. Her daughter reeled slightly from the blow, but stayed where she was, her chin defiant. Thinking of the broad circles Walt's hand made on Linnie's back the night Marcy caught him tucking her in, Marcy smacked the other cheek just as Paula reappeared at the door, bag of shampoos and sprays in one hand, jug of kerosene in the other.

Paula said quietly, I had this stuff left over from last time Tommy had it.

Marcy did not answer. She simply sank into a chair and opened her arms to Jake, who hadn't stopped crying since she'd put him down.

The Mississinewa dam bridge cracked and was closed for good that day. Paula helped Marcy wash and comb the kids' heads and vacuum and disinfect stuffed animals, beds, carpets. She daubed kerosene into the soft white hollow behind each small ear, sweet funnels Marcy'd once whispered love words in. Paula swiped her kerosened thumb across each brow. She shampooed Marcy's head and Marcy shampooed hers, gently rubbing Paula's scalp. Paula hugged the children before she left, but did not look Marcy in the eyes, did not say anything quilted and kind to help Marcy bear her grief.

After the kids were asleep, Marcy stripped the sheets off the sofa bed and put fresh ones on. She changed into a clean nightgown, the one she wore all day having been stained and sweated on. She picked up the *National Enquirer* and started to read. Putting the magazine down, she flipped on the small television set only to have Reagan's face appear. She turned the set off. She turned the light off. She stretched her arm out in the moonlight. She let it hover over the empty bed. Then she stuck her arm down the crevice and found the bottle, sat up to empty it in the dark of the room.

Marcy did not wake when Walt opened the door, nor when he staggered down the hall, nor when he pressed his heavy weight on her like the rain that broke the house.

But Linnie did. When Marcy finally opened her eyes, Linnie was standing in the doorway in a white nightgown. Ghost daughter. Girl who would not forget, who would always know drowned crocuses, water crashing down to flood the kitchen, dead kitten whose bones finally rose to the surface of the yard, her father's face when she told him about Walt and her mother, and what she did not tell: Walt standing at her bedroom door, one arm hanging on to the top of the doorframe, his other hand stroking at the back of his neck.

But this is about Marcy, who did not see Walt leave, either, who woke in the morning to find Walt gone, her bed empty but for the baby. Then the bruised feeling came in the center of her chest, the scream between her ears. But looking out the window to the edge of the yard, Marcy saw, through the rain, faint green buds on the trees. He would be back.

THE RIDE
[*Hog*]

Some girls are in it for the drugs, or the sex, or because they can't go back to the lives they left behind. Some love the language, the fast signs tossed off the handlebars as we pass each other in the blurry heat of the road, the secrecy, a religion better than the ones we had as kids.

Some of us love how easy the life is, everything stuffed in the saddlebags, our panties washed in motel sinks and dried in the wind. Some love the parking lots: twenty, thirty, sometimes hundreds of us pulling up, dealers, body-artists, old queens plugging for a day's turf, orange, pink, and green rags wrapped over their sun-bleached hair.

But in most cases, it starts with some girl falling for some guy she believes will finally settle down, like this Mandy chick who's been crying in the bathroom all night long in Tucson.

She knocks on our door around two. We let her in, her top torn, her mascara streaked.

Can I crash? she asks. Mike and I had a fight.

Sure, we say. We been there. Done that.

She shuts herself in with her big leather purse. She turns on the faucet, but we can still hear her talking to herself, preparing quiet threats, flushing the toilet again and again.

I try to sleep through it the way I slept through my parents as a child: I imagine the wide road before me, the bike beneath. While almost any roady'll tell you loud pipes save lives, lots of guys miss the fact that a ninety-mile-an-hour wind in a girl's ears blocks out all other sounds just like silence does. The rumble numbs the nerves.

At four in the morning, Danny flips over and pulls the pillow over his head. For Christ's sake, he mumbles. Seriously? Then he falls back asleep.

At first light, I open my eyes to see that Dixie's in the same position on the other double bed two feet away, Cedar's hairy arm thrown over her waist. She's looking at me, too, and we both sigh. I put my hand out and she clasps it briefly.

You want to go to her or should I? she says.

It's obvious to those of us who've been around the block a few times on the back of a Hog that Mike'll never stop dragging the country, that he's like Dixie's Cedar or my Danny.

Except I don't love Danny. I'm in it for the ride.

Don't get me wrong. I love the lots and the leather. I even love the motels with burned-out signs, rough white towels that smell of bleach, the single-serve coffee in little round filter packets. And when I say I don't love Danny, what I mean is that if he were a plumber or a even a banker, say, and he came home every night and we sat on the back porch picking our teeth and watching the grass wave in the back forty, I'd wear out on him real quick. And I suppose he'd wear out on me, too, despite that in the two years we've had he's been a tiger.

Can't get enough of you, he says.

Still, I'm far more likely to come on the interstate in Iowa— the deep thrill of green and tassel of corn, wind on my neck, sweat trickling between denim and spine—than with Danny banging around above me in the corner of a dank room in Little Rock or Flagstaff, say, on the kind of furniture picked up from the town dump one month and dropped off again the next.

You're better at it, I say to Dixie.

So Dixie goes in and tries to set this girl straight on what is what and who wants who and who'll make which sacrifices in our world. I've heard this speech before. And the failed arguments against it. But this Mandy chick just starts wailing again, which can mean only one thing. When I walk into the room, she's holding out a plastic stick, waving it around, pointing at it.

You got your choice, then, Dixie says firmly.

Dixie's only thirty, but she's a real biker queen with a long red Viking braid and a voice like a man's. All the boys call her Mama. They come to her for advice and she smacks them back into shape if they're beating on their old ladies or getting too caught up in the party.

Meanwhile, I'm quiet, vanilla-looking. Most of the guys I've hugged, the men whose leathered shoulderblades I've rested my head between as they ripped up miles of highway, have been surprised at how much I love it. And I have indulged the virgin fantasies of these men: picking up some small-town girl who's never felt the rumble. A girl like this one standing in the bathroom with her sweet round wet cheeks.

Dixie takes Mandy in her arms, presses her against her breasts, muffling her sobs so I can hear the guys talking about pancakes and eggs in the next room. I look down at the pile of torn open boxes and sticks, all of them bearing little pink pluses, a series of crucifixes rising from the small metal trash can.

So it goes.

We roll in. In a few hours, a makeshift town arises in the desert. Folks peddle their wares. The tattoo guys set up their guns. Some young queens get into the same shit they would have gotten into back home: they go on food runs, clean off picnic tables if it's a state park. They put out a good spread—usually hot dogs and potato chips and beer. Then they stand over it all like their mothers stood over their fathers—like they're in a house with wood paneling and a bottle of valium in the bathroom mirror like my mother always kept.

The men examine and labor over their own bikes and the bikes of others. They cross their arms, purse their lips. The bikes determine the pecking order, generally, and when that fails, there's always the fistfight broken up by other guys. After, the fighters stalk off or hug. Today's no different than any other, until Mandy shows up.

She unhooks her legs from some old guy's bike, a pity ride, no doubt, to see that Mike's got some local chick pressed up against his bike, his mouth moving against her ear. So Mandy runs off to the cinder-block bathroom. Dixie and I shake our heads.

Girl keeps up this way, she'll spend half her life in a toilet, Dixie says.

Cedar goes over to Mike and says, Cool it, eh?

Mike, though half Cedar's size, gets right up in Cedar's face, likely to impress this girl with her lanky blonde hair and buck teeth. Mike stays at it, forces Cedar to take him down. He shoves him to the ground and spits, Learn to pull it out once in awhile, eh? Cedar shakes Mike hard, once, twice, and stands and walks away.

Dixie laughs, welcomes Cedar to press himself against her, bear hug her and lift her.

A certain kind of guy will stay out of it all because, of course, what he really loves is the ride, too. That's the kind of guy Danny is. He's more likely to chill out on his back in any patch of green or sand soon as we get in. Today he's playing with the kids of the has-beens who drive over in their Buick station wagons and Dodge minivans and such to get a glimpse of what they've lost.

I have a lot of sympathy for these folks. The first two times I ran away, my parents sent the cops after me. They sent me back to my small bedroom in that small trailer to wait out high school, to take the job behind the counter at the grocery store or Wal-Mart, to get married to a millworker. I ran again, and again, until I was old enough to run for good.

When Mandy comes stalking back from the bathroom with a gleam of purpose in her eyes, Dixie and I are sitting on a picnic table with our plates on our knees, set up perfectly to watch Mandy's first turf fight brewing.

If a girl doesn't love the ride, or the sex, exactly, turf is usually why she sticks around. The turf fights are almost like sex, anyway: two sparring queens leaning against the still sizzling bikes of their men in summer's fields, maybe in Wyoming, loosestrife and ladyslipper blooming at their ankles. They suck on their cigarettes, size each other up. An old queen rips off her shirt and throws it in the dirt to reveal a leather bra and a lunging golden-orange tiger on her tanned but crumbling midrift. She pushes her sagging breasts in threat up against a younger queen, tall and lanky and muscled as a man.

Stay off my man, they say. But they mean so much more: This here something is *mine*, and mine alone.

Some girls will follow their man, his money, his coke right down to the end of themselves. Don't get me wrong. I love the stuff. Who doesn't want some love running down her throat? To be touched inside? And anybody pressed so close to another in travel needs a foot or so to herself.

But Mandy doesn't understand the rules, the way it's a game, and not for keeps, the way we women love each other even if we ball someone else's old man. Mandy pulls a gun, nice little Chief's Special, out of her big leather bag, holds it out in her trembling hand.

Dixie dumps her plate on the ground and starts to run, but I freeze.

Before Dixie can get to Mandy, she presses the trigger. I feel something wet splatter against me and I close my eyes. Everyone is silent—it's like those moments when Danny'll just stop the bike at night in the middle of nowhere, that silence that surrounds you, chills you, eats you up.

The silence is broken by a chuckle. Then another. When I open my eyes, I see that Mandy's burst a plastic bottle of Heinz on the picnic table.

By the time she pulls the trigger again, Danny has knocked me off the table and thrown himself over me. From the ground I can see Mandy getting a handle on the gun, pointing it directly at this poor local girl who doesn't even have the time to be shocked.

She pulls the trigger just as Dixie tackles her. The stray bullet lodges itself in the tire of somebody's minivan. We all pause, waiting. A few of the girls cover their ears. But instead of bursting, the tire lets out a long frustrated sigh.

Everybody laughs again while Mandy struggles and wails.

That's what love'll get you. And that's what I love about my life: by the end of the day, the turf will be gone anyway, left in a cloud of dust for some dark motel room or another parking lot or the house of another has-been who's left the road.

For good this time, they always say.

They'll be back, we say. And they almost always come back. Or he comes back alone. But usually, we'll pull into a parking lot two months later and see them, sheepish or proud to be back on their bikes, or we'll pull into the driveway of their house only to find the windows broken and no one there, nothing in the fridge, eviction notices littering the walk.

It was time to move on, they say.

Other girls stall when it comes time to move on. But I'm always as antsy as the men. And Danny loves that about me. He rolls me around on the ground, still cracking up.

Let's go, he says, wiping his eyes. He knows I don't want to hang around long enough to see the cops take her, call up those memories.

You bet, I say.

Want to steer? he asks.

It's our old joke. The thing with Danny is that he doesn't have these hangups. He really will let me drive if I want to. But I don't want to steer. I haven't seen the country, neither. *It's* seen *me*: the wide Mississippi covered with clumps of golden pollen, the bridge over the Ponchartrain, the thumb of Michigan, and, of course, Sturgis, South Dakota. But more than I love Sturgis I love the ride in—the Badlands coming from the east, ghosts of the dead rising out of those crags in the full moon, and from the south, in the sandhills of Nebraska, old monsters slumber under that blanket of grass, waiting, waiting.

But Danny and me on that Hog, we fly by so fast, we're clear in the next county by the time anything evil begins to unfold itself. We're gone before we can even start to be afraid.

TETHER

[Town & Country]

God put his hand down right here on this land, our grandmother told Cody the summer he came back from juvey dead behind the eyes.

At first it seemed my brother was simply in shock, roughed up by the cops who returned him, who forced his long body up the walkway, slapped that tether on his leg. But two weeks later at breakfast, when I passed Cody the milk, he just cupped the carton in his hands, stared at the flecked formica of the kitchen table and said, Thanks, Bo.

He didn't pour.

I walked down the stairs into the basement of our grandmother's house in River Rouge. I stood between the twin cots where Cody and I slept. Yellow sunlight streamed through the high rectangular window. The rumble of a train came up through the ragtaggle tiles my uncle had spread over the concrete floor when we first moved in.

I put my hand on my brother's pillow, in the cave left by his head. I felt the slight ridge of feathers that betrayed the dent in his skull, the force of the blow, the story that had emerged in night-sweaty fits. I let myself pray and cry. Then I quit both, began to plan how to save him.

&

Two years before, in April, in the morning before school, our breath hanging in the still frigid air, Cody coached me to bobby pin the battered old Town & Country our aunt left in the yard when it quit on her. He gripped my fingers and repeated the slight tapping motion until I got it, felt the quick metallic give in the lock like the startle of an animal.

Try it yourself now, he said.

I pushed the sharpened bobby pin into the hole, jiggled it, tapped. The shaft popped up out of the maroon vinyl.

Hot damn, he said, impressed, tugging on the earring in his right ear. Hot damn.

Cody was fifteen and big like our mom, but at ten, I was small for my age and choke-shouldered like our father. I'd never been in any trouble. No one would suspect me. No one would even notice me. I could probably go right in and do it in broad daylight, or at least at dusk. Then I wouldn't need a flashlight, which called too much attention to the process. That was where Cody kept running into trouble. That and the timing, the way folks seemed to notice him if he paused in the street, even if he held a cigarette like he was just having a smoke.

Will you give me a hand, Bo? I got to get somewhere tonight.

After dinner, when I was supposed to be playing hide and seek with the cousins and neighbors, the other kids whose families had remained after the last round of layoffs, Cody hunted the streets for a car he thought no one would miss, a car he got a feeling about.

He felt these cars out the same way he had always been able to feel deer asleep in a stand of trees back in Monroe. Some early November mornings in that year before we left our land he let me follow him into the cornfields. Steady as a man, he cradled his shotgun, dropped to his knees, and crawled soundlessly through the rows on his belly to get closer. I tried to be quiet, too, scraping the strip of flesh between my belt and the bottom of my outgrown waffle shirt against the bent husks as I crawled behind him, but I always managed to put my elbow on a snapping stalk. I could never make out anything in the trees from that distance, either. But sure enough, as we lay in wait, a deer, sometimes even a buck with a rack that made Cody inhale light and quick, ambled into the clearing. Cody took his time, aimed, double-checked, and killed it clean.

Up in Rouge, I wasn't just a tagalong. I was the henchman. Once Cody found the right car, he sent me in to do the lock. Later, when everyone was asleep, he climbed out the basement window, opened the unlocked car easily, ratcheted the steering wheel, hotwired it, and went joyriding. I waited and waited in the dark of the basement for his return, but I always fell asleep, woke with my neck sore from craning my ears toward the exact space on the street where I'd stood earlier, trying not to tremble as I did it.

I begged him to take me.

I get caught at something like this, Bo, that's one thing, he said. You're another.

He'd put on his Sunday clothes, comb his hair carefully. He took Uncle Bud's old army bag, wore our dad's United Steel Workers hat, the one with the bullet knick on the brim. Cody grinned, and then hoisted himself up and out.

&

The trouble with my brother was that he remembered every loss, not just his own, but the ones that came down in his blood, too.

An early memory: Cody holds my hand while my father stands in front of my mother, pleading, demanding. The money will mean so much to us boys. It will change our lives.

Her granddaddy come up from the hollers, paid for our land with his sweat, and no one's gonna take it from her. My mother cracks the 12-gauge open against her thigh, loads it, and takes aim.

They're going to take it, anyway, Charlene, my dad says, his voice shaking.

Over my dead body, she says, and presses the trigger. A Bud can rises sudden like a bird coming off the crooked sawhorse at the edge of the yard.

My brother drops my hand and runs over to her. Let me shoot one, Ma, he says. Let me.

&

At first, Cody was careful. He didn't take cars from our block, and he ditched them along the railroad tracks a good ways away. He didn't do it more than once a week. He always came back the next afternoon, right around the time he'd have gotten home from school anyway.

Then, suddenly, in May, he was gone for three days, had Grandma wringing her hands and Dad pacing the walkway.

When he finally returned, my dad took the belt to him even though he was far too old for it. They made him promise not to do it again. But he had things he had to tend to, he told me.

Come on, he'd say, holding up the bobby pin, There's a Camaro on First Street.

He always came in fresh and alive, waiting for my father's belt like it was kittens licking him. He grew a beard, did pull-ups on the basement pipes in his spare time, hardly ever wanted to shoot hoops.

Everybody said Cody had a girl somewhere. That was the kind of boy he was before they returned him to us with the bridge of his nose humped, wrists rubbed raw, his earlobe split into a snake's tongue.

&

Every morning that long summer he got back, after she swept the rust from the porch, my grandmother kept vigil with my brother there at the edge of his world—that cold-cracked slab of concrete bordered by streets with jagged tarry scars, reedy yards knifed with FORECLOSED signs. The train wailed. Cody shifted, that thing on his ankle clanging against the iron bench when he jiggled his legs. Our grandma's sweet but mislaid litany bounced off his skin, prison-colored, frogbelly. No horizon. A hundred degrees in the shade.

This here place is touched, she told him.

Bullshit, I said, just loud enough for her to hear. I spat on the driveway, threw Cody's old basketball against the faded blue siding of the house, the *tang!*-bup, *tang!*-bup echoing in my ears, the sweet sting of returning rubber on my palms. Out in Monroe, there had been no place to bounce a ball, and we never watched the game. But when we first came to Rouge, we practiced all the time, learned to play as well as the boys, black and white, who'd always lived in a paved place.

Bo, come on over here, now, Grandma said.

I rested the ball in a crack on the driveway so it wouldn't roll toward my father lying beneath the Town & Country. Uncle Bud leaned into its open hood. I couldn't tell if they were making progress, but I kept my fingers crossed.

I climbed the steps, wedged myself in on the bench next to Cody. Grandma rubbed my shoulder with her rough hand, twirled my rat-tail over her fingers. She tugged Cody into her side like a baby or a stack of newspapers. Flakes of black paint from the bench stuck to his pale thighs or fluttered to the porch. I knew what was coming.

She had proof. Astronauts had taken pictures from outer space. She pulled the wadded magazine page from her shirt, opened it, and smoothed the crinkles to show us the familiar green-yellow boxing glove punching at the blue-black lakes.

See, she said, He's got the whole world. And He's got ahold of it by Michigan.

We were lucky.

If you could see Port Hope, the way the afternoon light leaks out of an old barn in Kneeling, a field of corn in Tuscola county, even the eternal flame of Zug Island burning in the purple sky of dawn, maybe you'd believe her. I'm the son of her son, blood of her blood. But I'll tell you this: I came up in a place whose people have no luck, just demons that circle them their whole lives until they are closed into the deaths thought up for them before they were born.

&

When I was six and Cody was nearly eleven, we came in from playing to find our mother taking her sewing shears to her hair, the floor and her shoulders a mess of gold-honey.

Why, Ma? Cody said, touching her stubbled head, a spring cornfield crushed by long snow.

We're at war, son.

He nodded at her solemnly.

A month later, Dad moved into Grandma's. I rode in a shopping cart while mom and Cody collected canned goods to stock the cabinets, fill the cellar. I helped them gather fallen branches, rotten boards and tractor tires from the old barn to build a fence around the property.

Come on, Bo, Cody said. Hurry now.

I ran behind them carrying the tall green lamp from the table between our beds, the cord tangling between my legs. Together, my mother and my brother hauled the headboard of the queen bed my parents slept in. I didn't really understand the urgency that ran between them, but I felt it, real as the tension of that long brown cord Cody snapped from the lamp. He used it to lash the headboard to the trunk of the old cherry tree and the mailbox, blocking the driveway.

There was no fortress like that to protect Cody when they came after him. They followed him right into the house that night, yelling, pointing their pistols and their flashlights. My family stood dream-faced in the hallway, my grandmother in her nightgown, her hands up. Cody escaped out the back door. They caught him in the alley, pressed his face to the ground in a circle of light. They lifted him by his shoulders, dragged him away.

No one handcuffed me. They assumed that I was the innocent bystander I'd always been. I circled my wrists with my fingers, imagining how it felt, that clamping down and my life changing for keeps.

&

While we sat on the porch listening to our grandmother's spiel about the glories of the mitten state, Uncle Bud's boys, Randy and Dean, ran laughing into her yard, their jeans dusty from the railroad culverts we all wrestled around in despite the movies they showed every fall at school: legless children who'd played too close to the tracks, their weeping mothers and lucky brothers. In black-and-white, a train would barrel down and barrel down toward all of us sitting cross-legged in the dark school cafeteria but tied to the tracks, too, a voiceover talking velocity and suction, the way it could pull you under, strong as a tornado—right up until the last minute, when the film cut to a kid's regretful face, his shirtsleeve pinned up over his missing arm. Or his grave.

Boys! Grandma called, and Dean and Randy clomped up the porch steps, gathered around to look at her photograph.

Cool, Randy said, winking at Dean.

Yeah, Dean said.

See? Gram said to me.

I nodded, but I stared at the page, at the lower knuckle of the Thumb, where Ontario reached out around the heart of Lake St. Clair, the thick vein of its river, to touch Detroit, River Rouge, Del Ray. The city was grey, empty, grassless—a living thing turned to stone.

See there? she said to Cody.

Can't go nowhere, he said. Like he had just remembered and couldn't believe it. Like if he could go just *one* other place, it wouldn't be so bad.

&

After my father signed the papers, the nuclear plant put up a real chain-link fence around my mother's makeshift one. They began construction on the new towers. Our house joined the ones around it, boarded and empty. Dad paid off all his debt and my grandmother's house, too.

When he came for us, my mom took a single shot, grazed the brim of his USW hat.

On our early visits to the state home where they sent her, my dad went to my mother's room first, his ruined hat clenched in his fist, but of course she wouldn't speak to him.

Then Cody and I went in. He sat next to the bed and held her hand while I hung back. They whispered together, her face like a child's, until my dad came to take us. Then she clutched at Cody's arm and said: Promise. Promise your momma.

I promise, Cody said.

Dad sold her out, Cody told me again and again in the basement, sold our land. Bastard went to court. She never even got to defend herself.

Neither had Cody. In fact, no one had talked much at all. Even the rapping of the judge's gavel was muted, as if we were under water.

What else could he do, Cody? He couldn't feed us without money.

No, Bo. You got it wrong. You can't feed people without land.

The next winter, Michigan closed half its homes, and our mother was moved. The following year, she was moved again. We never went to visit her in that home.

I extracted myself from the bench, walked into the yard and picked up the basketball. I cupped it in my palm, mimicking God. I made a sound like wind rushing just before a storm, pushing the ball always just ahead of where it would have fallen. Dean and Randy cracked up.

I went back to throwing the ball against the side of the house. The Pistons had ended the season on a losing streak, but Cody didn't care anymore, hadn't been there the nights I sat alone before the fuzzy black-and-white TV in the damp basement watching, sending the game to him like a prayer.

My dad slipped out from under the car and said, Bo, give it a rest, wouldja?

I pushed the basketball through our window, watched it bounce around the room, knock into the duffel bags I'd stuffed with T-shirts and sandwiches the night before. The ball rolled into the lamp, which tipped over, the lightbulb smashing on the floor. I shrugged. What did it matter? With any luck we'd be gone by dark.

The train wailed again. It was the third one I'd counted since dawn. I looked at Cody to see if he was going chicken, but he was blank. His pinky finger itched at the sweat that trickled into the tether, which wanted to swallow everything of my brother, even the smallest things.

&

Before I understood how it worked, it seemed easy enough. If it was just the tether that needed to stay in the house, we'd break it off.

Won't work, Cody said, but he let me try.

He sat hunched on his cot, his head tipped slightly to the side, watching as I gripped the box and took a pair of wire cutters to the black plastic bracelet. They came down hard on the metal that went all the way around inside.

Upstairs, I heard the phone ring. My grandmother's voice came echoing down. Cody?

Yeah, he said, almost a question, but flat, as if he already knew what she'd say.

It's your parole officer.

He pushed me away gently, stood. I followed, stayed with him as he answered her question: I guess I must've bumped it up against something, he said. I'm right here'n my house.

He turned around, tears in his eyes. See, it ain't never gonna happen, he said.

We'll find a way, I said. I promise.

&

I want to meet the girl, I said to Cody the middle of June that year he screwed up. Or I ain't doing any more cars for you, I said.

He grinned at me and twirled the basketball on his forefinger.

I ain't, I said. I don't care if you beg.

By then, Cody had grown less careful, and a lot of people suspected him. But in Rouge, folks kept an eye out for each other and against outsiders. And because we lived on what had been a white block before the layoffs, we heard plenty of grumbling about the riffraff from Ecorse coming over to squat in the newly abandoned houses and stealing cars. But Cody soon exhausted our neighbors' loyalty. Someone finally called the cops, who came asking questions. After that, Dad and Uncle Bud began to stand sentry outside our window nights.

There ain't no girl, Bo, Cody said, laughing. But here's a deal, he said. You get them off our backs, and I'll take you with me tonight.

Fine, I said, grabbing the ball from him.

There's a blue Galaxie parked on Jefferson, he said. She's old, but I think she'll do.

That night after dinner, I said loudly, Will you take me to shoot hoops, Cody?

I don't know, little brother, he said, pretending to be too busy for me, which both infuriated me and made me want to laugh.

Please, Cody.

Well, I ain't supposed to leave the house, he said, and both of us looked at Dad.

Please? I begged.

Fine, then. Be back by dark?

Sure, we said. Sure thing.

&

As the sun went down, we left the park and snuck through the alleyways together to the Galaxie. We stayed low, ran through the street, and crawled in the passenger side.

Cody tossed himself into the driver's seat. He pulled the small crowbar from the army bag and popped the steering wheel like a pro. He twisted the wires fast and easy between his fingers and the car roared to life. Before anyone could look out the window and see us, he jammed the gas pedal and we tore down Jefferson, skipping the first three stop signs.

Cody made a few turns, and we were on the highway. Once my heart stopped pounding, I rolled down the window and rested my arm on the door just like Cody. He turned the radio on and lit a cigarette. The music and the cool night air and smoke washed over me. The night got darker. There were no strip malls and no factories. Then it hit me. I recognized where we were the way you'll recognize your own face in the bathroom mirror in the middle of the night, startled at how you could have forgotten its shape. The towers of the nuclear plant rose up before me.

Cody turned the headlights off, drove through a secret cut in the chain-link, and navigated around the remains of my mother's fence. He pulled up to what was left of the old house. He hopped out of the car. I got out slowly, my legs shaking. He pounded on the roof of the Galaxie.

See? he hooted.

I squinted. I saw that part of the roof had caved in right over my old room where there had always been a water stain—bound to happen—and the windows were boarded up and dark. But then a flash of light pierced the darkness. I watched it bounce from window to window.

Don't be scared, Cody said.

I followed him to the side porch. The planks creaked beneath our feet. He took a key out of his pocket and put it in the door handle. We walked inside. There, at a makeshift kitchen table propped with cinder blocks, was my mother, shuffling a deck of cards, smoking a cigarette, too, her hair thick with snarls. She rested the flashlight in a noose that hung from the ceiling and held out her arms. I went into them, sweet with relief and sick with the smell of her.

How? I said, pulling away, incredulous. How?

Cody walked over to a small cooler, got himself a beer, and sat down with mom. They played a game of rummy so casually as they told the story: week after week, with a fake I.D. in his pocket, Cody had driven north in the night, slept in the backseat of whichever car he had stolen, visited my mother in that hospital unfit for dogs. Posing as Dad—that was why the stupid beard and hat—he made play with the staff, and as soon as he had their trust, he signed our mother's release forms. Took her into family custody, he said. Easy as pie.

Pie, indeed, my mother said.

As they spoke, the house seemed to warm up behind us, fall back through time to become the house it had been five years earlier. I felt like myself again. I asked to be dealt in.

We left at two in the morning. Cody took the back way. I felt light over the rises, dizzy in the cornfields, wild, free, as if nothing would ever stop me again from claiming what was mine.

Then I saw the flashing lights behind us, red and blue, red and blue. Of course, my brother, believer in any hope and all miracles, tried to lose them. As we tore through the night, all I could think was: they'll send my mother back to that place. I didn't even understand about Cody.

&

In the basement, we tried everything. A wrench, a saw. Anytime we screwed with it, the damned phone rang, Cody's parole officer. Anything strong enough to take that thing off wasn't fast enough. In the workroom, I fingered an old blowtorch. But that would burn his leg. Besides, we still needed a way to escape once it was off.

These were the things we talked about late in the night, our cots pushed close together, me staring at the split in Cody's ear.

We could just steal another car, I said. Drive it straight up to Canada.

He crinkled up his face. It will have to be better than that, I think, he said. I don't know if I can, if I can—he gestured hotwiring, the crowbar, then fingered the back of his head where they'd cracked his skull with a nightstick. He started to cry. You have to help me, he said. Please.

So I'm the one who did the figuring. Since I had no idea how to hotwire a car, we'd have to wait on the T&C. Once Dad and Uncle Bud finally made it cough and sputter, got it started, and headed to lunch, we'd throw our stuff in. We'd head for the train a quarter-mile away, in keeping with the schedule we knew by heart. I'd drive. I'd keep driving even when our family gathered on the porch, their mouths open. I'd even drive past my father, who ran into the street yelling, holding onto the side mirror.

&

Twenty years later and still the ghost of my brother's boyhood comes to me thick as the air of that summer, pressing constant. Or he comes sudden, the fast-remembered glimpse of a forbidden species poached and caged in a country whose name has since changed. His real pain is mostly forgotten, even by me, likely because in a world with real justice, I'd bear the lion's share. What I do bear is the truth of what happened, what I did. My sacrament of reconciliation is to show it:

I pull him out of the passenger seat and toward the tracks. I lay him on the ground and hold his leg steady, all the fierceness in my body moving toward the only solution I have. I press the hard box of the tether to the tracks. He watches the sky, smiles at it a little, like he's dreaming. I watch the train. I see the old leaves and dust blowing out and up as it gets closer. Then I see, I really see the way it sucks things back under, how the wind spirals up thick and is cut by the rotors. There's no one in the dead black eyes, but the brakes screech, snapping the small bones in my ears.

Out of the corner of my eye, I see my father running toward us, my uncle behind him, Dean and Randy, and in the distance, the round figure of my grandmother. My grandmother. When I see her I understand, finally. There is no magic that will save us. There's no logic either. I grab Cody under the arms and pull as hard as I can, yanking his torso away from the tracks. But the momentum of the train can't be beat. His leg bumps up sudden, like a reflex. The tracks and the train form a mouth that tugs at him like a fish trying the line, but he's cut loose before I can understand what's happened. Is the tether gone? Can we still make it out of here?

My father is with us now, rips his belt from its loops and I cringe away, covering my head, waiting for it to hit my back.

Nothing comes.

The train has stopped.

When I look up, I see that my father has looped his belt around what remains of Cody's leg and a black stain spreads in the colorless dust. Cody is looking down at himself, shaking his hands, screaming. Dad's got his foot pressed to Cody's thigh, and he's pulling on the other end of the belt. Before I can stand, before I can move toward them, my uncle's dragging me away. He presses me toward my grandmother, who buries my face in her breasts.

Uncle Bud says, I'll call 911. His voice is strange and tinny in my ruined ears.

Not the cops. Don't let them take me. And please, anything, but don't let them take Cody.

No one's taking you, my grandmother says. I realize I've been talking aloud. I want to run, but I'm too tired. Instead, I cry. When I look up, my grandmother's lips are moving. I pray with her until the ambulance arrives.

I'm still praying when they start to ask their questions: This was the kid who tried to stop it? His brother? He found him trying to—

That'll be enough, my grandmother says. It was an accident, that's all.

The woman from the ambulance finally puts the pill on my tongue and gives me a paper cup of water. Swallow, she says. I do.

&

Grandma treated Cody's recovery like any other wound one of us might have. She called it a setback. She took out the walker she had refused to use herself and made him get up on his good leg. After they gave him a fake leg that was almost the color of his skin, she helped wrap it to his stump, she told him to put weight on it. She shushed away his tears. You still got a chance, she said. You always got a chance if you're still breathing.

Luckily, they did not arrest him.

Slowly, almost imperceptibly, Cody came back to himself some, woke up. When the plants opened back up and took the younger guys in for half the price they'd paid our fathers, he put in an application. They hired him on the custodial crew.

He did alright for himself. Not in the way I did, but of course, my whole life was built on his back, something I never forgot. In quiet moments, as I stared out at the quad silenced by a light dusting of snow like we got down in Monroe, I missed the way it ridged up in the cornfields. There at my desk with the warm light glowing over my books, I'd feel the ghosts coming on, creeping up over my shoulder. I'd look around to see if anyone was watching, if they might be able to tell right through my skin what I came from.

When I found I was alone, I'd sometimes sit back and bring the ghosts on myself.

I'd think of how Grandma told us that damned story even on her deathbed, holding out her hand to show us how we were being held all the time, how we would be held even after she went.

I'd think of my mother living out the rest of her life straightjacketed, silent, alone, her eyes on the ceiling. How the last time I went to see her, she didn't recognize me.

I'd think of how Cody and I came upon a doe struggling on her back in the woods once, bullet hole through her ribs, but not enough to kill her. The way he shook his head. Said you should never leave anything to die in pain. Only if you were one hundred percent sure, he said, should you take the shot. Only if you could really pull it off.

THE BLACK BOX
[*Falcon*]

It's actually orange, Mitch says, shaking the pills loosely back and forth like dice in his palm. Did you know it's actually orange?

No, I say, turning off the old TV. The torn body of the small plane flickers and disappears from the screen. I see my torso in its grey reflection, a pinpoint of white light left briefly in my center.

The first morning storm of gunfire echoes from the edge of the cornfield. It's the season of the flight of the hunted, the missed escape into the wide South Dakota sky. I pause, listening for the baby. A whimper. Then silence. Melt dripping from the eaves. I cup my aching breasts.

Mitch stares into his hand. He looks up at me.

I take a bottle from the windowsill, open it, count the pills inside. No, he hasn't already taken his morning dose. I touch his arm and nod.

Mitch tosses the pills into his mouth and gulps a glass of water. A shadow passes over his face as geese clot the sky, darken the windows. Mitch opens the kitchen blinds. The tiny bodies of the hunters, nearly a mile away, walk through what's left of the snow. They gather the dead.

I know Mitch is thinking about my brother. Francis, or Frank, as we started calling him once my father was dead, loved to rise early, put on those brown pants patterned with fake reeds and stalks, set decoys.

But the first time dad took him hunting, Francis came back bawling. He didn't know the birds would die. That shooting them would kill them. My father cuffed him in the back of the head as he walked up the porch steps.

Sissy.

I sip my coffee, which Mitch can no longer drink, and I should not drink, according to the pediatrician. But I was up all night. My first date since Jared was born. Six months without fucking. Over a year if you count being pregnant.

It's so they can find it, Mitch says, so they can see it in the wreckage.

He wraps his robe around his bloated torso, reveals his calves, the muscle weak on the bone. He's not even thirty.

He picks up two bills from the stack on the counter. Frank's, he says.

I sigh. We can barely stay afloat as it is. The drugs are expensive. Mitch can't work anymore. He shouldn't really sit with Jared while I'm at the diner either, let alone all night. Eventually I'll have to hire a sitter. And that will cost, of course.

Let me guess. Forwarding address unknown?

Let's go back to bed for awhile, Mitch says.

I look at the kitchen clock. It's after six. We're supposed to be at the doctor at two, and it takes four hours to get to the city. I should shower, make sandwiches, pack the diaper bag.

Sure, I say.

Let's get the baby up and bring him in, too, Mitch says, grinning so that his dimple comes out.

Ok, I say.

A baby has a whole lifetime to catch up on sleep.

I have to run to the bathroom, Mitch says. He points to his stomach, rolls his eyes, tucks the dark hair that's fallen into his eyes behind his ear.

I nod.

In the small room that was my brother's growing up, and mine while I was pregnant, I lean over Jared. When I was in labor, the nurse told me that seeing his face would be like seeing the face of God. This morning Jared looks more like a revolutionary, arm thrown up over his head, his fingers curled in a fist. I touch his cheek. He turns his head and opens his mouth. I put my finger lightly on his neck, touching the small red birth-stain.

Another round of gunfire sounds and Jared starts, begins to wail. I gather him to my chest, feeling guilty, like I've cheated on him. I'm still wearing my dress from last night. *That* black dress, Mitch called it when he pulled it from the closet. The dress that would get me laid even if my nipples leaked the whole time. And they did, because it was Mitch who got up at two in the morning and gave Jared a bottle while I was lying on my back in a stranger's bed, staring at the ceiling of his small apartment, hoping that Mitch indeed remembered to feed Jared, wondering how soon I could get up, take my full breasts with me, start the long drive home without seeming ungrateful. How I could pass through town before light broke so no one would see me.

I carry Jared and my coffee to the bed Mitch used to share with my brother, the bed my mother used to share with my father. I crawl in on what is now my side, the floor littered with books and magazines. I trip over *Reading Your Baby's Emotions*, whose blurb claimed that if I could listen to his cries correctly, I could avoid Jared ending up on some shrink's couch complaining about how bad I screwed him up. On Mitch's side, *A Natural Guide to Living With HIV* is perched over the alarm clock, blocking the time.

Jared and I lie in the light pouring in from the window. I pull my dress down, put my nipple in Jared's mouth, abruptly silencing his cries. These are the things, the invisible things, that move from one body to another: viruses, love, caffeine.

Mitch comes in, pulls off his T-shirt. He's burst a new blood vessel in his eye. He stands for a moment, dazed. He says, Don't know why I bother. I can never keep them down.

I invite him with my arm to curl around us.

When Jared is through, I pull my dress up, put him on Mitch's naked chest, shrunken, concave. Jared's feet kick on Mitch's swollen belly.

I'd forgotten until last night, burying my face in the thick muscle and fur, what a healthy man's body looks like. And it was Mitch who set me up.

This Reiki guy I found, Paul, is single, he said. *Cute. And straight. A little Carnie. Just your type.*

What the hell is Reiki? I asked. Three months later, I know Reiki, I know Yoga, I know Tarot. We're trying anything these days. Mitch says Reiki works the best, that it feels like Paul can find every lurking virus in his brain. Doesn't look that different from the laying on of hands to me, my mother's church.

On the days Mitch couldn't be trusted to drive, which was most days last month, I dropped him off at Paul's office. Paul asked me about dinner every time. Until I said, *Yes. Sure. I'll come to your place for a drink.* He'd had no idea what he was getting into. But he held me when I cried.

I turn over, burying my head in what used to be my brother's pillow, wondering if Paul, as a Reiki guy, could feel what is left of Frank in my skin when he touched me. Or in Mitch's skin. Or maybe even Francis is buried somewhere inside, still running into my arms, saying *I'm not a sissy.* I wonder whether those who dance somewhere between the living and the dead leave a particular kind of energy, something in the shape of a question mark, in the ones who wonder where they are, or *if* they still are.

I don't realize I've fallen asleep until I wake up to Mitch washing dishes and Jared wailing. It makes me think of what death might be like, the way you disappear from yourself without knowing it. I pull the book off the alarm. It's past nine. We'll be late.

I strip off my dress, get in the shower. Water runs down my body. My middle is heavy, strange and new. I wrap myself in Mitch's robe and brush the tangles from my hair. Mitch brings Jared, who has worked himself into a frenzy, to the bathroom. He suckles while I apply mascara. I won't have time to make sandwiches, but Mitch can't hold down lunchmeat or yeasted bread these days, anyway.

Mitch is packing Jared's stuff in the next room, muttering to himself, Three bags for one kid on a day trip. What a queen, what a queen . . .

I hold Jared up and laugh, touch my nose to his. He wrinkles his face in a smile, as if he gets Mitch's joke. I pull on a sweater and jeans, juggling Jared from arm to arm, which I am getting better at. He can stay in his footies. It's cold out, despite the sun. He'll fall asleep in the car, anyway. Mitch is already outside and I don't want to leave him too long. These appointment days get to him, make the panic of losing memories worse.

The phone rings in the next room, and abruptly stops. Frank?

It rings again. I stand over it, Jared on my hip. I consider answering. The familiar wound of hope spreads in my chest. Then I laugh. What would I even say? I wait for the machine to click on.

As I'm walking out the door I hear Paul clear his throat, say he'd like to see me again. I wince. He sounds so sincere.

I navigate baby and bags around the hole in the front porch that we still haven't had fixed.

We have to take the old Falcon Frank left in the yard because Mitch's is a pickup, no room for a carseat, and my old Honda needs new tires. When I lean over to strap Jared in, I catch a faint whiff of Camels and pine. Frank's smell. Lingering after almost a year. I imagine telling him—*A plane crashed early this morning, there were no survivors*—

That sucks, he'd have said at fifteen, leaning against the counter, lighting his smoke. Or, *bummer*.

And somehow this seems deep to me now. But in every memory I have of him—even if it's from when he was small, digging with a metal kitchen spoon in the yard, looking up just in time to watch my father knock my mother off the front porch with an elbow to the nose—he's the junkie he eventually became. He's got purple half-moons under his cornflower eyes, loose teeth in bloody gums, pocks and scars right along with his muddy knees, nose running and tears. He's desperate for another wad of crank, asking for money. He's slamming an old crowbar down through the wood of the same porch. Holding it up against me. Mitch is standing between us. Frank is weeping. Stomping off into the darkness.

Fuck you, Sophie. Fuck yourself.

I can drive, Mitch says.

You sure? I ask.

I feel fine.

I pause.

Sophie, he says. Let me do it while I still can?

Jared is staring at me from the hood of his snowsuit with his wide brown eyes, his mouth working his pacifier. He falls asleep before we've gotten to the end of the driveway. I try to settle in, but I can't relax because I am afraid the next memory to go will be how to use the brakes. Silly. Mitch turns the car onto the main road. The hunters lift the geese by their necks, toss them onto the piles in the beds of their trucks. One hunter turns toward us, smiles and gives a small wave, more like a salute. Mitch waves back.

Nice, he says, pulling his hat down against the sun's glare on the windshield.

Yeah, I say, turning around to look at the hunter's long lean body.

We drive for two hours, watching the flocks, white on the horizon, black in the air.

Mitch says, I hate to say it, but I think I could eat, now.

The cocktail makes him so sick in the mornings, so sick most of the time, that we have to take his stomach up on it anytime he thinks he can handle food. Soon after Frank left, we drove to California for a rally. We had to stop every hour so I could pee and search for a restaurant that sold lemon pie; lemon was all I craved when I was pregnant. Mitch held my hair while I puked in truck stop bathrooms early in the morning. Then we stood with our feet in the Pacific. On the crowded sidewalk in San Francisco, Mitch threw himself down while I leaned my belly against him, traced his outline in chalk, left it to be blurred by walkers until it looked more like the ultrasound photo we held up to the light in our hotel room at night, outlining Jared's tiny penis. A boy.

We'll make it quick, he says. He pulls off the interstate. We choose a diner where he can get french fries, which seem to cause less upset than anything.

We stand behind the Please Wait To Be Seated sign. A television behind the counter blares the news. *The reason for the plane's descent has not yet been determined.* Firemen dressed in blue protective suits walk into the smoldering wreckage to excavate the dead. I turn away. As if he, too, has been watching, Jared turns his face against my shirt, resting his cheek on my heart.

You all need a high chair? the small blonde waitress asks. She winks and pinches Jared quick and light on the cheek. He smiles, flirting back. I never do these kinds of things at work, and don't understand fully the waitresses who do, who seem to love serving coffee and wiping formica tables.

No, Mitch says, and to me, I'll hold him.

Jared will cry if we put him in a high chair.

I'm not a sissy. I'm not a sissy.

We follow the waitress to a booth and settle ourselves in, Jared over Mitch's shoulder. A woman with tight blue curls in the next booth opens her mouth and widens her eyes in fake surprise, trying to make Jared laugh. Her husband shakes his head, embarrassed. I know their type. Lunch before noon. Big spenders. Fifty-cent tip.

What can I get you all? the waitress asks.

French fries and a Coke, Mitch says, rubbing his five o'clock shadow against Jared's head. A few honey-colored strands cling to Mitch's chin.

You? she asks.

The same, I say. And can you bring water?

She walks away, pinching Jared's cheek again, which makes me want to punch her.

Mitch takes a bottle from the pocket of his flannel, checks the time, and hands the bottle to me to open. I do, and he takes it and tips the pills into his mouth just as the waitress delivers water. He drinks.

The woman in the next booth says loudly, I remember when ours were that little.

I nod.

He sure looks like his daddy, doesn't he Charles? says the woman.

The man grunts his agreement.

Mitch smiles at me apologetically.

The man who gave me Jared passed through town once, has never seen him, doesn't know he exists. Mitch hasn't had sex with a woman since high school as far as I know, least of all me. But there's no reason to tell that to this woman with a silver cross hanging from her papery neck.

The waitress puts our fries and Cokes on the table. Mitch jiggles Jared and coos at him. I pour ketchup on my fries, offering none to Mitch because it burns his stomach. I listen to the snippets of news that float over from the bar. *Four passengers, no survivors.* I think of the mothers of the men on that plane, the sisters of the boys. At least they'll know what became of their men.

After the waitress clears our plates and brings the check, I head to the bathroom with Jared so I can feed him. Mitch is close behind, headed to the men's room. He staggers a bit, puts his hand on his stomach.

You got it? I ask, as the man exiting the bathroom brushes past us, lifting his pants by his belt and scowling.

If people don't know, they assume Mitch is a drunk. That it's a beer belly. That's why the women in town pity me now instead of hating me, instead of whispering *slut* behind my back. They think: *She went and ended up with a man like her father. Poor thing.*

Got it, Mitch says. I'll meet you back in the car.

The old woman is in the bathroom, too. She's putting on lipstick far too orange for her skin. She watches as I pull down the plastic changing table, remove Jared's diaper.

Your husband's so sweet with that baby, she says at her reflection. In my day, the men didn't do too much in the way of the babies.

I don't know what to say to this, and she's obviously waiting for some kind of response.

He's not my husband, I say, tossing the shitty diaper in the trash.

I don't say: We're not married and we're on our way to Minneapolis, where we can look at options besides AZT. The cocktail. Death.

She turns toward me as if she'll reply, but she doesn't. She just purses her lips and leaves as I seal another diaper around my son's solid frame. I sink down onto the floor, resting him in my lap. I feed him, watching his small hand knead my breast.

I walk out of the bathroom, ignoring the stares of the waitress and the old woman, who are leaning together over the counter, whispering excitedly. The man from the bathroom stands by, having obviously added his two cents. If only they knew the half of it. My mother was like this, too. Let any girl from town show up at the grocery store with a round belly, no husband, and she was on the phone in ten minutes, sharing the news. She was all for the laying on of hands.

I wrap Jared's snowsuit around him loosely, close him in my coat, too, and walk to the car. I settle him into his seat with my face burning. Mitch is in the passenger seat, defeated.

What's with you? Mitch asks as I slam the door.

Assholes, I say, pulling the car back onto the highway and then the interstate.

As always, he replies.

As I merge into the left lane he asks, How was it with Paul?

Fine, I say, feeling a careful silence well up in my throat.

You think you'll see him again?

No, I say.

He nods. Too bad, he says. He's a good guy.

I just don't need the hassle of it now, I say. As if I ever do.

Jared cries all the way to Minneapolis.

Mitch says every few minutes, Take it easy, buddy. Take it easy. Mitch turns around in his seat, but can't get Jared to take the pacifier. He pushes it out again and again with his tongue.

My father insisted one year on driving all the way to Washington, D.C., to visit Arlington Cemetery and the Vietnam Memorial. We stood before the wall of names. My mother prayed, her head bowed, her lips moving so fast I hoped God had a good ear. I was ten; Frank was eight. The rows of graves looked like decoys set up for the kill.

Who cares?

I'll make you care.

I want to turn on the radio. Plug my ears. How will I do this without Mitch? I'm driving on the shining road and I don't want to stop in Minneapolis. I want to keep driving, take Frank's old route, go to the ocean, show my son the ocean. Find my brother. Show him my son. But we're crossing the bridge in a city where bridges collapse, getting off the interstate edged with grey snow. And the reality is that my brother thought I was crazy for wanting a life that looked anything like our mother's.

If I were you, Sophie, I'd get rid of it.

We arrive at the University hospital with five minutes to spare. I park the car, change Jared's diaper in the backseat, while Mitch runs in. Despite his red and tear-stained cheeks, Jared seems to love the elevator we take all the way to the tenth floor. We join Mitch in the waiting room where he's mulling over *Healthy Choices Magazine.* Two men sitting cross-legged in designer jeans and sweaters stare at him in his flannel shirt and khakis, his hands rough and stained from years of work at the mine.

This says we could let him wean himself when he's ready, says Mitch. He reads aloud: Most babies will wean themselves at one year or older.

Easy for you to say, I laugh. They aren't your tits.

Mitch cracks up, and the two men frown.

A nurse pops her head into the room and says, Mitchell Rawling?

That's me, Mitch says.

I can see he is trying to be brave.

Can I take him? he says to me, gathering Jared in his arms.

I follow my missing brother's lover and my bastard son into the examining room, while the two men stare at me. One of them pretends to examine his perfect nails when I stare back.

I settle myself into the chair while the nurse takes Mitch's blood pressure. Jared watches the cuff as it puffs up on Mitch's arm. He gives one of his little guffaws, his new laugh that comes from deep in the belly, as the cuff deflates again.

Any changes to your symptoms? the nurse asks.

Just more nausea, he says. Weight loss. Some tingling in my hands and feet. But mostly it's still the memory loss.

She jots this information in Mitch's chart, clicks her pen, and stands. The doctor will be in soon, she says and leaves the room.

I want to take his chart, throw it out the window, let it fall to the pavement, be swallowed by the river in this city to wash up on its banks years after. Like the time-capsule Frank buried in the yard. I don't remember what he thought was so important then. He dug all those long spring days in the worn patch of dirt near the front porch, dug until he could stand waist-deep in the hole. Then he buried in a painted wooden crate whatever it was that made up that year of our lives, the screaming, the accusations, the time our mother spent weeping on a church pew, strange men touching her skin. Frank was supposed to retrieve those memories, but he never did, so he never had to know that year again. I imagine someone bending on the banks of the river, finding Mitch's chart, opening it, knowing the truth we'd never have to know.

I join Mitch on the examining table, wrap my arms around his shoulders from behind. I bury my face in his neck. Kiss my son.

I miss him, Mitch says.

I know, I say.

It's not working, he says, the Cocktail.

I know.

And I'm worried—

Yeah?

I'm worried that I'll lose him, lose what I can remember—

Good. I don't say it aloud. Because none of it is Frank's fault. Not the drugs, not the virus. There are too many memories, too many mornings of Mitch waking to an empty bed, an empty wallet. And there is a hole in the porch. And if I could erase those things, I would.

Mitch shakes his head quickly, blinking back the tears that have come. You know about the hummingbirds? he asks, changing the subject, looking at Jared.

No, I say.

Well, these scientists were wondering how the hummingbirds made it all the way from Mexico to Canada 'cause they're so small. They found one of these geese right around here and guess what was tucked under its wing?

What?

Stowaways, he says.

I imagine being tucked beneath a warm wing.

The doctor comes in, a tall man with straight brown hair. Mitch raises his eyebrows. *Told you so.*

What have we here? he asks.

Mitch lifts Jared by his torso, holds him up. My nephew, he says.

Mitch seems so young to me in this moment, seems like the boy he was when Frank first brought him home, senior year of high school for me, freshman year for them. He moved into my brother's room. My mother was gone by then. My father was clueless. I was the only one who knew.

Beautiful boy, the doctor says, and holds out his hand to me.

Patrick Reynolds, he says, introducing himself.

Sophie, I say, squeezing his hand, which is cool.

He sits down and opens the file. He thumbs through it, clears his throat. That always means bad news. Your last viral load test revealed an increase, he says, sighing.

Yes, Mitch says.

The virus is mutating all the time, of course. A new strain—some cases in New York City, L.A.—is resistant to the anti-retrovirals. And—

I stop listening. New York. L.A. Of course. All the time Frank spent in the cab of a truck waiting to get to a place where it was fine to want what he wanted. But by the time we get what we want in a life that has told us not to want, it is usually too late for us.

What then? Mitch asks. I mean, what now?

A treatment interruption could be useful—sometimes the drugs become less effective over time. Only the strong mutations survive, so rotation can help.

And if not?

Dr. Reynolds doesn't have to answer. No one knows. Everyone knows.

And what about my memory?

The doctor shakes his head.

We're silent in the elevator. We walk out into the bright sunshine. Jared squints his eyes. Mitch looks at the sky.

So blue against the red brick, is all he says.

Before we leave the city we stop to fill the car with gas. Mitch says he's going to go get a pack of smokes. What does it matter? He strides from the glass doors with his hands already cupped to his face lighting his cigarette. He blows a plume of smoke into the cold air.

I drive on the way home, taking the highway instead of the interstate. Jared sleeps. Mitch turns on the radio, no doubt hoping for the weather report. Anything mundane. But a fuzzy voice intones: *The migration of the spring geese, which often cause complications for larger crafts, appears to have been the cause of the crash. The occupants likely died before the plane descended.* As if this is some relief. *It looks like none of the components remained intact. The wreckage has left a large crater . . .*

A hole in the ground. Like a six-year-old digs? Like a grave? Like a body opening for birth? No, much bigger. And what of the stowaways? Mitch closes his eyes, tries to rest. Goddamnit. I adjust the rearview mirror to look at Jared. His head is thrown back, in sleep. I see the birth-stain. *A sign,* my mother might have said. Is he breathing? I turn the radio off. I tap the brakes, listen. I can hear his breath.

We are driving past the wreckage. From the road we can see the search for warm bodies has ended. All that remains is the hope of memory and the knowledge of what happens in the last minutes of life.

Let's stop, Mitch says.

No, I say.

The sun gets heavy on the horizon, changes the sky to blood, then disappears. I drive through the dark town where my brother wandered with a crowbar in his hand. *Why bother getting tested?* Frank said. *Can't do nothing about it.* Except smash windows. This I would not erase. My brother shimmering in a street full of broken glass.

And I can see from a mile away that the lights are on in our home, a car I don't recognize parked in the yard. I brake at the corner and look at Mitch, who shrugs. But I know he feels a surge of hope tingle in his gut, too. Maybe Frank is sitting with his arm over the back of the couch. Probably watching TV. Drinking a Michelob.

I park the car and run up the porch steps. I burst into the house. I turn the kitchen corner. I slam full-force into another body, grab it, and the arms grab back. I look up.

It's Paul.

Where's Frank? I ask.

Who's Frank?

My brother? I say.

Paul holds me at arm's length, looks down at me. He sucks in his bottom lip. Oh, he says.

Oh, I repeat softly, covering my mouth.

Of course it was Paul's car in the yard. Paul whose hand is gently encircling my arm.

I thought I would surprise you, he says.

Behind him three glasses of wine wait on the table. Candles burn. The house smells warm, full, like it used to when my mother made Thanksgiving dinner.

I knew it was going to be a long day and I thought— He clears his throat. Well, I thought . . .

Mitch comes up behind me, Jared asleep on his arm.

I'm sorry, Paul says.

Mitch grins. Uh. I'll put the baby down.

Paul makes a move toward his jacket and shoes, but I grab his arm. No, I say. It's ok.

I made dinner, he said. Chicken.

Sounds good, Mitch tosses over his shoulder.

Paul says, I'm so sorry.

It's not your fault, I say, feeling myself grimace.

I hate it when strangers see my grief. Especially strangers I've fucked. Ones who just might be clairvoyant. I pick up a glass of wine and sit at the table.

Mitch emerges from the bedroom, draws his hand across his throat. The boy is out, he says and heads to the front porch for a smoke.

The three of us sit in the kitchen and laugh and talk and eat as if Mitch has not been handed a death sentence. As if there will be survivors, not just thirty minutes recorded, the random chatter of life, then the explosion of feathers and bones hitting the windshield.

Later, after Paul and I have made love in my parents' bed, I lean on my bent arm and look into Paul's face. His cheekbones are high and fine.

Did you hear about the hummingbirds?

He shakes his head, no.

So I tell him all I know and he listens, staring into my eyes.

Josie Sigler

Sweet, he says, burrowing his face into my neck and kissing. But have you ever seen a hummingbird go? he mumbles. They could make it on their own power, I think.

He puts his hand on my leaking breast. Maybe my mother was onto something with the laying on of hands. Maybe God *is* a revolutionary, leaving the reading of the signs to us. And maybe I will find a way to make my love keep.

But first I will rise at dawn, take my body from Paul's, feed my son in the first light. I will put Jared back to sleep with Mitch on the couch. I'll go outside and take up my father's shovel. I will break through the still-frozen ground to find the wooden crate so carefully built, to smell the faint must of what's left: The bird, nothing but bone and feather, eye-hoops dainty as engagement rings. And next to the skeleton, a decoy with a black X on its back.

So she won't be lonely, Sophie.

I hear the baby cry from deep within the house. It's time to go in. I toss dirt back into the hole, bury my brother, the one who came through this field carrying death in his arms.

A MAN IS NOT A STAR
[Silverado]

A man does not set himself on fire.

A man works. Strapped to the ceiling, dangling over a half-made truck, he welds, he solders, twelve hours, fourteen hours, weekends, overtime.

Thus, he is tired at day's end. He does not lie awake, waiting out the dark hours open-eyed and jittery, shocked by the few quick splashes that haunt the bridge of his wife's nose, headlights from the rare car out in this weather—folks coming home from the VFW hall a mile up the road.

A man enjoys a beer. His first beer, he enjoys the most. Twelve years old. Pabst on tap. Bunch of old drunks leaning over card tables, slapping him on the back. The women biting their Virginia Slims Menthols, hugging his boyish face to their breasts. His father's hand ghosting itself on the chilled mug and the beer was so smooth—

Or was it bitter?

Yes, that's right. Before he was a man, he had looked around that hall and silently vowed never to go to war. He couldn't bear the thought of losing a leg, the terror that rose in him whenever he saw the strange pattern of burns that moved down his father's back like red-bellied snakes in a fallow cornfield—

No. A man is courageous. He is willing to fight. Sometimes he is just born in a good month, has the right letter beginning his last name, misses the draft, lands himself a fine job.

But this is not how a man's memory works, the truth slipping back and forth like that painting thick with blue and yellow paint.

Painted by a madman, his wife had said.

Of course, a man pays no attention to art, and his soul certainly does not slip a bit in his chest over a damned painting. But maybe he could make an exception for this guy, crazy or not, who had captured so exactly the landscape of his youth, the blurred lights of distant smokestacks rising up beyond the hills, blazing in the night.

Those are *stars*, his smallest daughter said.

A man knows when he's bested. He could have simply replied: Sure are.

Instead, he shrugged, turned his too-clean hands up and stuffed them useless into his pockets, wandered off. When no one was looking, he tore the painting out of the magazine and filed it deep in his wallet.

A man does not tremble in the dark as he extracts himself from a woman's arms. He pulls on his old white tube socks, union suit, grease-stained Wranglers, flannel, UAW hat—Local 594, Pontiac Assembly Center, used to be Truck and Bus in the good old days. A man loves these clothes even if a woman hates them, even if she's wished for him in a suit and tie or even in one of those faggy black turtlenecks the guys in her art magazines wear with pleated beige pants.

Though she might tell you otherwise, a woman born and bred in Michigan loves a Big Three Man, the black-crusted half-moon fingernails, the life-line on his palms a telling river of oil. A man like that can always reassure a woman. He never has to tiptoe away like a criminal. A loser. An idiot who could have just gone ahead and enlisted like everybody else, gotten his balls all full of Agent Orange. If he'd survived, he'd at least have benefits to offer his family. Something besides the life insurance policy sold to him by that shiny-faced guy who went door-to-door.

A man does not dream up accidents, no matter how much nothing he finds turning out his pockets.

Before a man leaves the house in the night, he checks on his girls. His youngest has crawled in with the middle girl on the bottom bunk.

Their faces are pressed together as if they have been telling secrets.

The middle girl loves to dance—at least, she used to love it, wandered around in a tutu most of her second-grade year. He took her to the VFW hall with him once—a secret he knew she'd keep from her mother. There, he twirled her, taught her to do the Achy Breaky Heart. Now she's dyed her hair green and wears nothing but the tattered black T-shirts she's scavenged from her brother's closet. She looks like a mourning leprechaun and he tells her so.

Goddamnit, now. A man stands beside the women in his life, does not leave them to fend for themselves. A man pays for their weddings, sends them to college. He's worth more alive than dead.

He looks at the face of his oldest daughter, the one who dreamed of going away to school but settled for some classes up at the community college. Because a man never thinks about what he takes from a woman, he's erased the memory of that desperate year when everyone was out a job—Flint was closing—and this girl sat awake with him like a woman at the table in that small trailer at four in the morning while her mother scrubbed the floor of an office building in the city, trying to make up the difference.

He was drunk. He cried.

A real man walks his girl back to bed, tucks her in with a glass of milk—real milk from a jug with a red cap, Vitamin D fortified, not that powdered crap issued by the state. He tells her to have sweet dreams even if worry and loneliness drown his heart.

He hardly knows this daughter now. She is for another man to know.

A man might pause briefly at his son's empty room. He does not lift a white undershirt to his nose and inhale, trying to get at the musky smell that remains in the cotton. He picks up his boy's football and tosses it up in the air to watch it spin and come neatly back to his palm, but he does not hold it in the crook of his arm and think of his boy as a baby: sweet-faced, too kind to murder anyone, even for his country.

He presses the button on the fire detector to make sure the green light still flashes, but he does not send its small bleep echoing through the hallway until his youngest girl moans for him to stop.

A man takes pleasure in passing through the door to his garage.

It's just your standard door, but it leads to his own world. And at least once a week he's entitled to fiddle at his workbench or sit in a green plastic yard chair amidst the junk cars, wound up orange extension cords, and old power tools. A man smokes and sips whiskey, warms his feet by the small kerosene heater, listens to the old country songs his girls hate. Hick music, they call it. A man knows he's not a hick. He's not an alcoholic. He's worked hard in his lifetime. Thus, a man has to have his space. He can't have his foreman screaming in one ear and his wife in the other twenty-four seven.

A man does not hunt the shelves frantically and nearly weep to find that he gave the last of the kerosene to the neighbors. Everybody's hurting. It's a man's job to make sure the people he knows get what they need. It's a man's job to solve difficult problems. He'll have to take some canisters up to Larry's. It's the Super America now, open twenty-four hours, but before that it was just Larry's, open 'til ten.

He emerges from the side door of the garage carrying in his flanneled arms two old gas canisters from his boat, one of them slightly dented, a crease in the red paint that bothers his thumbnail. He stares into the snowy sky, suddenly remembering those barn kittens his brothers did that autumn long ago—

No, he was never so green, a virgin in his thirteenth spring, and helpless. He was never thin enough to fall in with the young saplings at the pasture's edge where he watched his brothers hold those late summer kittens by their tails and dip them into a bucket of gasoline. The kittens mewed and arched their terrified backs.

Don't do it. Please.

He'd never beg like that.

Surely he admired his brothers' rippling arms as they hefted the burlap sack. They said the kittens would be like balls of fire rolling down the road.

Hot damn.

A man does not hate his brothers for their cruelty, even if his girls do hate them, even if the middle girl, upon hearing this story, says she'll never talk to Uncle Buddy again. But a man can't hold a grudge against a guy whose wife hasn't given it up for years. A man does not think: If I were his wife, I'd sleep in another bed, too. Kitten-Killer.

This is the equation between father and daughter: He protects and cares for her. He asks nothing in exchange. He swears he'll murder anyone who hurts her. And maybe he does it, too.

A man does not leave a house full of women for two years and his son barely sixteen, even if General Motors says: it's that or lose his job.

This middle daughter, the one who looks most like him, was eleven when they forced him to take the transfer to Baltimore. There, a lost bird, wounded, flew onto the balcony of his shitty apartment where he lived by himself. He set its wing, nursed it back to health. A man does not believe the bird was his daughter's spirit calling him home to save her. When he's returned to his family and takes his girl on his knee only to have her cringe away, a man gets angry about what happened to her, not scared.

Tonight his breath is a cloud in the air and his truck—beautiful Silverado 1500 extended cab, half-ton, American-made—leaves tracks that will soon be covered by more loose white powder. He takes the back roads where he taught his boy to drive. A man loves the moment his boy understands the release of the clutch and the pickup chugs violently forward.

It was spring, then. Everything was green.

A man does not imagine the moment his boy's shaved blonde skull is destroyed by shrapnel, grenade, bullet. It's probably the middle of the day in Iraq and his son might be driving over some gravelly dusty road, maybe thinking of him, too. It's hot and sunny in the desert and a man who believes in his country and its power has to believe his boy is safe because his boy has always been brave. Courage, a man thinks, leads to surviving any risk. A man is proud of his boy, weapons of mass destruction or no.

His boy was the only person who understood how close they had come so many times to losing everything. These are the things with which a man trusts a son: layoffs, bankruptcies, strikes, the houses that seemed to slip through his hands like so much sand. A man can admit this much of the past: the harder he held to any life, the faster it ran out, and at the last moment, when it seemed he had grasped something solid, it was skin on skin. But he tries not to think about the jobs he worked during the lean years. He's proud of how he and the boy managed things, but won't tell you about stints sweeping parking lots, selling vacuum cleaners, mopping floors right alongside his wife. Jobs you can't even find anymore.

The boy took up a Sunday paper route to bring in grocery money. That's a good boy.

But a man does not consider the days he came home, exhausted and dirty, to find his son, just thirteen, patching a hole in the roof or his daughter wearing an apron while her mother slept, all of them forging the signatures on the report cards and stifling their thick winter coughs in a chorus of grateful suffocation. He does not ask: what must that have been like? That childhood?

Some creep pulled his middle daughter into a car as she walked home from her dance class and opened her body. Her father was not there to gather her as the others in their sheer pink tights were gathered by their fathers. A man does not pretend this did not happen. He doesn't lock himself in his garage and drink whiskey. He doesn't rest until he finds out who he ought to kill. He remembers a particular pair of eyes in the VFW hall one of those twirling nights, a specific skinny punk playing basketball in the park. But a man does not look at other men and discover every single one is the one who hurt his girl.

He guns the engine. The white cloud that lifts into the air behind his tires might give him a flash of the compact his mother opened to take the shine from her nose in church. But the snow does not suddenly smell to him of incense—a kind of clean, washed holiness. The stars do not become her eyes, staring at him, admonishing him. A man does not remember how that swift drift of frankincense clung to her even as she walked out into a bright Sunday afternoon. A man does not bury his face for just a moment in the grey curls that peek out from the green silk kerchief. He does not suddenly hold his mother with an urge strong as sex to press her birdlike ribs against his cotton T-shirt.

If she dies the next morning, if her body lies on the floor in the hallway for three days before he stops in and finds her, a man is allowed a field or two of open grief. But no more.

Paused briefly at the junction where he'll turn onto the highway, even a man will admire—just briefly—how the snow's weighed down the long broad arms of the pine trees so they are like his mother was too, carrying so much but still standing, still moving toward him. A man doesn't ask: What would she think if she could see him now? Were her sacrifices worth nothing to him?

And his father! Second Infantry, Indianhead Division. His father was pushed face down in a pile of muck along the Yalu River in Korea, taken prisoner. His old man didn't lay eyes on him until he was three years old. A man does not admit that he was scared of the strange soldier who limped up the driveway from the mailbox. That he is still scared of the man who thrashed him for forgetting to latch the gate to the hog pen, for spying on his sisters, for crying when Sister Margaret rapped his knuckles because he insisted on writing with his left hand. A man admits he had it coming. He had it coming every time it came. His old man did the best he could.

Having endured the cherry-hot pincers that left the scars on his back, his pops should not have had to endure, too, raising a son fond of watercolors, a quiet boy who loved to sit in the corner of the kindergarten class and stare at A Child's Introduction to Art. A father should not have to tolerate a boy who cried like a baby when his brothers played some stupid prank with a bunch of useless barn cats. And if a father does get stuck with such a son, why would that son subject him to this final insult? This final sissy act?

And what about his own son coming back from Iraq to find—
No.

A man wouldn't even think about this. He would not, in fact, think of any of this—except perhaps that his father was a hero for having endured Death Valley and it means he is a hero's son even if he did not sign up to go to Vietnam.

A man swings his legs from his truck, feels the slight crunch as his feet sink into the unplowed parking lot. He is full of pride, not shame, as he walks into the station, shakes his sodden boots off on the mat and greets an old buddy with a slap on the back.

Ain't the same, he thinks, now that the Super America come in and razed everything, got rid of the porch and the salvage out back. The old men in UAW hats who read the paper there, too, seem to have disappeared.

A man rolls with the changes.

He doesn't use *grief* or *fear, insomnia* or *depression*. He says his balls are still on midnights after all those years of taking what he could get.

He doesn't say *unfair*. Those fuckers who buy foreign, he says. Fucking gas prices and President Fucking Bush.

Larry says he thinks that's the real name his momma give him.

A man says, Bailouts or no, I'm getting raped.

Larry asks how the boy is over there.

A man nods, tightens his lips. The boy's holding up. He's carrying fifty-six pounds of gear on his lanky frame through the Iraqi Desert. A man can face the footage—thank God on CNN and not their local news—in which his boy—he knew it was his boy right away—kicks the body of a dead Iraqi. For sport, the reporter had said. Sport. A man doesn't whine, even to himself: What else could my son do? What choice did my boy have? He says: That's what war can do to a man. It changes a man on the level of the blood. A father simply accepts a fiercer son, one whose face revealed his pleasure, not his rage, as he slammed his heavy foot into that body.

Larry cracks a beer even though it's past two in the morning. A man pounds his friend on the back some more—nothing in the world as good as putting beer on your whiskey—and drains the Stroh's to the can's bottom. He could ask Larry for more whiskey and Larry'd surely pony it up, but only if a guy'll say something about why he's here in the middle of the night. Fight with his wife. Trouble with the neighbors. No time for fishing. But a man cannot tell an old buddy the truth. He can't turn to Larry as they come back in through the milk crates and toilet paper and hold him and say that he just can't take it anymore.

He says his garage heater's out—he's trying to watch the replays of the game—asks about the kerosene.

Them red cans are for gasoline. Can't letcha fill 'em with the kerosene, buddy, Larry says.

You shitting me? he asks.

No way no how. Super America rules.

Crock of shit, a man says. But he takes this in stride like a man

Josie Sigler

would, chooses gasoline.

Careful with that, Larry says. Can't use it in the kerosene lamp.

But a man can do most anything the packaging of an appliance warns you not to do. And he does not think: Bingo. The insurance company will eat that up like candy.

Go home to your wife, now, asshole, Larry says.

A man, after carousing, returns himself to a woman who stood by him while other families were broken by layoffs and shutdowns and fear. He forgets all of those things that could have sent a jagged crack into their union, wakes in the morning, drinks a hot cup of coffee. Maybe he buys some nightcrawlers and tries his luck in the lake. But after that, what does he do? What does he do if there is no place to make cars?

The first time he peered under the hood of an old Model-T, that tangle of rubber and metal was more familiar to him in a glance than his own innards and veins, more familiar than the women he loved in that car paid for with his own barnyard sweat every Sunday. And once he bought it, he was a man. A car was what made you a man. A man, everyone's got to understand, cannot just sit around with his union suit hanging out of his jeans and watch The Geography Channel all damned day.

A man does not, as he hauls those stinking canisters into the garage, merely shrug when his woman appears at the door in her tattered grey robe to ask: It's midwinter. It's the middle of the night. What's the need for gasoline, now?

She's thinking it's the house he's going to do.

A man takes her in his arms, says, I would never risk that. We're going to make it, a man says. He tells her they were out of kerosene. His feet were cold.

A man does not get nervous when she rests her hand on the small green aluminum boat as if she's going to stay awhile. A man is never forced to sell his real boat, the one that carried him far enough out into the blue to feel he had escaped, to claim a dented patchling like this one. A man's boat has his own wife's name on the side and its tiny engine is not rigged to the gunnel with a coat hanger. His boat ranks up there with his truck, his tackle, his favorite wrench.

If a woman persists in her Why now? stance, a man tells her that it's just an Irish errand, as his mother always said when she did something he could not understand.

A man kisses his worried wife's forehead, and sends her back to bed.

He does not stare for long hours out the window from his seat in the garage. He's made to last. He's like a rock. A man makes a truck and drives the truck he's made. He smells of the factory—oil, grease, sweat—where he has worked for thirty-one years. He believes the great American automobile will rise again.

He might tease his sweet and ruined daughter as she walks through the garage just after dawn, all gelled up and ready for school.

She might say, Anything wrong, Dad?

Not a thing, he says. He smiles and rubs his hand over her spiked hair, asks why, when God give her such nice hair, she's done the shit she's done to it.

Even though they both know why, a man and his daughter laugh.

A man simply does not do this thing in front of her, his bird who doubles back, worried.

He does not give his youngest this constellation as she cries and pounds on the glass of the garage door leading to the kitchen and screams: No.

Nor does he do this in front of his oldest—a man does not offer her this dream, unforgettable, burned onto her eyelids for the rest of her life so that she never sleeps again without seeing it: this flailing, spinning, screaming angel of fire whose wings rise suddenly into the rafters.

A man does not do this to a woman who loved him when he was down to nothing and fed him and his children and in all the years he's known her has never once hurt him or them nor complained. A woman who smiled every time she felt him watching her in the dark.

A man does not do this—

But he's not a man, anymore.

Freed from all the rules he's ever known, he bolts his side of the garage door. He wails as he would have his entire life if a man were

Josie Sigler

allowed to wail. He opens the cap on one of the canisters and holds it over his head. He pours and shakes his hair, the way his murderer son used to do with water between plays on the football field. He even opens his mouth, letting the gasoline coat his tongue, sting his nostrils. It soaks him, trickles down into his shoes. Because he wants to be sure of this thing, he empties the second canister. He makes sure the kerosene heater gets a good dose and stands before it. He takes up a match.

They are behind the glass of the door. Their eyes and mouths beg. His wife brings up her fist wrapped in the sleeve of her tattered terry-cloth robe to break the door's glass, but not soon enough. He wants to stop, let her save him again. But they'll be better off without him.

He strikes it.

A man would find another way. If he were a man, he'd be sorry. But if he had a whole town, he'd be the thick yellow moon in the sky. He'd never waver. If he painted himself, he'd be the bright star rising above the trees and he'd sail right over everything that's left here.

Author's acknowledgements

Many thanks to Tabitha Morgan, Cody Todd, Naira Kuzmich, Lelania Avila, Benjamin Shockey, José Navarro, Emanuel Powell III, Robert Keteyian, Alexis Lothian, Janalynn Bliss, David St. John, Dana Johnson, T.C. Boyle, Catherine Ratliff, Bill Handley, Saba Razvi, Bryan Hurt, Rande Daykin, Becky Buyers, Jeff Key, Anne Marie Claire, and Rhona Klein for reading early versions of these stories and saying they were better than a poke in the eye with a sharp stick. Thanks to Aaron Kier, Kathlene Postma, Mary Rockcastle, Miciah Bay Gault, Claire Guyton, and Mary Crockett Hill for editorial suggestions in regards to the original published versions of these stories. A special thanks to Taylor Grenfell, Mindy Chaffin, Susie Henderson, and especially Jennifer Sibara and Catherine Ratliff for proofing the final version. Your suggestions, support, and friendship made these stories loads better than they were when I first scratched them out.

Thanks to my grandmother, Dorothy, for letting me play with her old calligraphy set for hours as a kid. Those tubes of ink and nibs made me want to write before I could even spell, and the gossip at her kitchen table taught me tons about dialogue, character, and plot.

Thanks to my parents, Cheryl, George, and Jerry, who like to sit around a summer fire and listen to these tales and tell me what sounds true and what sounds like "a load of B.S." You are responsible for my sense of humor and I'm very grateful for that.

A special thanks to my sister, Jeanné, who inspired "The Last Trees in River Rouge Weep for Carlotta Contadino," and my brother, Jeremy, who gave me the seeds that grew into "Deep, Michigan." I am so lucky we were born into the same family.

Thanks to Karen Waldron and Bill Carpenter for putting me on my path as a younger writer. Every writer should have teachers as generous as you were to me at seventeen years old.

Thanks to the Wallis Annenberg Endowed Fellowship and the amazing, wonderful folks at the Sitka Center for Art and Ecology for providing funds and space and beauty and kindness.

Thanks to John for loaning me his GTO on a sunny autumn day in Portland.

Thanks to Joe Taylor and all the folks at Livingston Press—Elizabeth Brooker, Jim Carroll, Nelson Sims, Tricia Taylor, Danielle Harvey, Eadie

Caver, Carleen Davis, Connie James, and Joseph Seale—for believing in these stories and donating many hours to helping me separate the grain from the chaff.

And thank you, thank you, always, Jennifer, for being a partner so courageous and true. Your love makes all things possible.

author's photo: Jennifer Sibara

Josie Sigler was born Downriver Detroit and grew up in the Midwest. Her chapbook, *Calamity,* was published by Proem Press. Her book of poems, *living must bury,* winner of the 2010 Motherwell Prize, was published by Fence Books. Josie recently completed a PEN Northwest Margery Davis Boyden Wilderness Residency, which affords a writer the opportunity to live and work on a remote homestead near the Rogue River in southern Oregon's Klamath Mountains. While so ensconced, she spent a good deal of time with a cougar who shared the same territory. Having survived that rare and spine-tingling friendship, she is currently in residence at the Sitka Center for Art and Ecology, where she is working on a novel and a new book of poems.